SHERRYL WOODS

An O'Brien Family Christmas

HARLEQUIN®

entertain, enrich, inspire™

Recycling programs
for this product may
not exist in your area.

ISBN-13: 978-0-7783-1391-5

AN O'BRIEN FAMILY CHRISTMAS

Copyright © 2011 by Sherryl Woods

For questions and comments about the quality of this book, please contact us at CustomerService@Harlequin.com.

www.Harlequin.com

Printed in U.S.A.

To the Outer Banks gang—George and Carol Sweda; Kristi, Ron, Donovan, Carson and Morgan Petrecca; Austin Luchowski; Kim, Jay, Adam and Jonathan Cerar; and Keri, Tom and Evan Krajewski. Thanks for all the great summer memories in the "big house"!

Dear Friends,

Welcome to another Christmas season with the O'Briens. If you missed it in hardcover, here's your chance to spend the holidays in Ireland with a family known for its Christmas cheer and romantic meddling!

Everyone's agreed that Matthew O'Brien and Laila Riley belong together—except Laila's parents and Laila herself. Will the magic of the season and the determination of a man who doesn't give up be enough to overcome Laila's doubts and her parents' objections?

As if the mission to get Matthew and Laila down the aisle isn't enough to keep the O'Briens busy, Mick O'Brien is also in a frenzy over his mother rekindling a romance with an old flame. Will Nell have a second chance at love, or will Mick stand in her way?

I hope you enjoy this journey to Ireland with the O'Briens. And I hope you'll be watching for the reissues of two of my older books, *After Tex* and *Angel Mine*, coming to stores in early 2013. The setting of Whispering Wind, Wyoming, may not be what you're used to reading from me, but I think you'll recognize the small-town charm and emotional stories.

Meantime, my very best wishes for the happiest of holidays for you and your families.

All best,

Sherryl

1

She'd lost the job of a lifetime because of a man!

Every time Laila Riley allowed herself to think back—how hard she'd worked to gain her father's trust, how desperately she'd wanted to prove herself capable of running the bank he'd established years ago in Chesapeake Shores, only to throw it all away for what had to have been the most ridiculous fling of all times—it made her a little crazy. She was not the kind of woman who did anything because of a man. She wasn't impetuous or flighty. She was better than that, more sure of herself, more independent.

She allowed herself a sigh. Surely she must have been out of her mind to think that she and much younger playboy Matthew O'Brien could possibly have a respectable future. That had to explain her uncharacteristic behavior.

But because she'd taken leave of her senses, here she was, back in a tiny office, doing the sort of accounting work that bored her to tears. None of the hoped-for jobs at other area banks had materialized. Her credentials were impeccable. Everyone had agreed on that. But in the current economy, no one was hiring at her level. If that changed, she'd be the first person they called. *Blah-blah-blah.* She'd seen the encouraging words for what they were—so many empty promises.

Within weeks of quitting her job in a huff at the family owned community bank, she'd started berating herself for her foolishness and resenting Matthew for his role in it. If only he hadn't been so blasted irresistible, she'd thought accusingly. So determined to win her heart. She'd been caught up in the romance of his pursuit.

Even as she was blaming him for all that charm and sex appeal, she was forced to admit that Matthew himself had been totally supportive in the aftermath of her impulsive decision to leave her father's bank. He'd even found—or created, she suspected—an accounting opening for her at his uncle Mick's architectural firm, but she didn't want his handouts. She no longer wanted anything from him, in fact, except to be left alone.

Correction: she wanted sex, but that was out of the question. Lust, combined with loneliness and envy for all the happily married couples around her, was exactly what had gotten her in trouble in the first place.

Ending their misguided relationship within weeks of quitting her job had been her only choice. If she'd also packed up and left Chesapeake Shores, it would have been the ultimate trifecta, a complete upending of her life.

But, no, she didn't quite have the will to cut the ties

to the town she loved and her infuriating family. So she was stuck here, alone and miserable and working for half a dozen pitiful clients who barely kept her in the Rocky Road ice cream that lately she craved by the gallon.

"Sulking, I see," Jess O'Brien Lincoln said, braving Laila's dark mood by stepping into the office uninvited. She looked around, took in the drab beige walls that needed paint, the tiny window with no view and the seriously scarred desk, shook her head, then sat on a chair that had seen better days. Not even the bright posters Laila had framed could save this place, and they both knew it.

"I am not sulking," Laila protested. "I'm working."

"Yes, I can see all the work piled up on your desk," Jess noted, her tone wry.

"It's on the computer," Laila informed her. "Haven't you heard? Financial records are computerized these days."

Jess tried to settle more comfortably onto the cramped office's one guest chair, gave up and shrugged. "So I hear. Not my forte."

Laila gave her friend a wary look. "Why are you here? I hope it's not on your cousin's behalf. I've told Matthew—"

Jess cut her off. "Matthew didn't send me."

Despite the convincing tone, Laila wasn't reassured. O'Briens were a sneaky lot. "Then what brings you by?"

"I can't stop in to check on a friend?"

"You could, but lately you've been so caught up in the extended honeymoon phase of your marriage that you barely leave the inn."

"Not true. I go out all the time. Will and I are not joined at the hip. He does his thing. I do mine," she declared with a nonchalance that didn't fool either of them. Once Jess had accepted her feelings for Will were real and his for her, she'd been a little gaga ever since.

"If you say so." Maybe it just seemed to Laila that everyone in Chesapeake Shores was traveling in contented pairs these days. "Okay, let's say I believe this is a purely casual visit. What's up with you? Is everything running smoothly at the inn?"

Jess's expression brightened. "We're packed, as a matter of fact. Connor gave me this idea a while back about offering specials for small business conferences, and now that the golf course has opened nearby, that's working out really well during the week. Even better, weekends are booked all the way through the holidays with tourists. The word seems to be out that the inn is a great spot for a romantic getaway. It helped that we had a huge spread in a regional travel magazine showcasing how beautiful it is here at Christmas."

Laila was genuinely impressed. "That's terrific. You should be proud of yourself, Jess. Making a success of the inn is a fantastic accomplishment."

Jess grinned. "Quite a change from my teenage screwups, huh? And that brings me to one of the things I wanted to discuss with you."

"Uh-oh, here it comes," Laila murmured, regarding her accusingly, "I knew this wasn't just some spur-of-the-moment visit."

"Okay, I'll admit it. I am on a mission," Jess confessed. "Two, as a matter of fact. One from Abby and me, and one from Susie. Neither one has a thing to do with Matthew, I promise."

Laila wasn't entirely placated. They were all O'Briens, after all, a family that was notoriously tight-knit. These days, she didn't trust a single one of them, not even her sister-in-law Abby, much less the clever friend seated across from her with the cat-that-swallowed-the-canary glint in her eyes. As for Susie, she was Matthew's sister, so her motives were suspect on more levels than Laila could possibly count.

"Okay, try me," she said grudgingly. "What do you and Abby want? And why didn't Abby call me herself?"

"She did. Several times, in fact. Apparently you haven't been returning her calls, or your brother's, or those of anyone else with the name Riley. Or O'Brien, come to think of it. Connie says she hasn't spoken to you in ages, and even though I'm a Lincoln now, you've pretty much been ignoring me, as well." She gave Laila a chiding look. "Thus the personal visit."

"I've been busy," Laila claimed defensively.

"Yeah, right," Jess replied, clearly not buying it. She waved off the subject. "We'll leave a discussion of the way you've been neglecting your friends for another time. This morning I want to talk to you about taking on the accounting duties at the inn."

Laila regarded her with deepening suspicion. Jess had started The Inn at Eagle Point, gotten herself into financial hot water even before the doors opened, and needed her older sister to bail her out. Abby, the family's financial whiz, had maintained a fierce oversight of the inn's accounting procedures and expenditures ever since. She'd put her own hand-chosen man in charge of keeping tabs on things. Jess had chafed at the strict oversight, but even she knew it had been a necessity.

"What happened to the accountant Abby brought on board?" Laila asked.

"He was okay, but it was time for a change," Jess responded blithely. "We need someone full-time, or close to full-time, anyway. Abby agrees."

Laila stiffened. "So, this change was your idea? Jess, I don't need your charity. I have clients."

"How many?" Jess asked bluntly.

"Enough."

"I doubt it. Something tells me your dispute with your father over Matthew affected more than your position at the bank. Your old clients have been slow to return, thanks to all the gossip. Am I right?"

Laila ignored the question. Jess clearly didn't expect an answer. She thought she had the situation pegged and, sadly, she was right.

Jess shook her head, her expression indignant. "I swear some people in this town are living in the Dark Ages!"

"Exactly as my father predicted," Laila admitted ruefully.

"For an idiot, he has way too much influence," Jess countered.

"Well, he was right about one thing," Laila said. "Apparently nobody trusts their money with someone who displays poor judgment in their personal life." She waved her hand dismissively. "Look, that's all water under the bridge. I've been networking like crazy the past couple of months. Everything will work out. You don't need to worry about me or make up jobs for me."

"But you're not so overburdened with work that you can't take on the inn, are you?" Jess persisted. "Tell the truth."

Laila sighed. "No."

"Then you're officially hired as of today. You can stay here in this charming space, if you choose to, or you can move into the nice, spacious office I have ready for you at the inn."

Laila wasn't quite ready to cave in. "What am I supposed to do, ditch the clients who dared to take a chance on me?"

"Of course not. You can continue handling as many private clients as you'd like to. I have no problem with them coming to the inn to meet with you." She gave Laila an encouraging grin. "There are windows, Laila. Big windows with a view of the bay. And that huge piece of expensive modern art that hung on your office wall at the bank? The one there's not even room for in here? There's a perfect spot for that, too."

"Now you're just taunting me," Laila said, imagining it. Currently that prized picture was gathering dust in a storage locker.

"All you have to do is say yes, and the office is yours, along with the job," Jess confirmed.

Laila's pride, which had taken a beating lately, kicked in. She started to refuse, just on principle, then chided herself for allowing emotion to overrule logic. She needed more work, especially if she was to keep herself sane. It had nothing to do with the income. She'd been frugal with her paychecks over the years. She could weather these lean times, at least if she limited her ice cream intake. No, it was too many empty hours weighing on her. She needed to fill them.

Lately she was spending way too much time thinking about Matthew, wondering if she'd made a mistake in cutting him out of her life once and for all. Those were the kinds of weak, mostly sex-driven thoughts that could prove dangerous.

Biting back the desire to refuse, she forced herself to nod, forced a gracious note into her voice. "Thank you."

Jess grinned at her, clearly understanding how difficult it had been for Laila to acquiesce. "You do know that working with me is no piece of cake, right? You won't be thanking me a few weeks from now. You'll be earning every penny of the generous salary Abby thinks we should pay you."

"I learned how to deal with you years ago, when you were nothing more than an annoying little brat," Laila countered. "I'll survive." Her gaze narrowed. "Maybe before I give you a final answer, though, you should tell me about Susie's mission."

"No big deal," Jess claimed casually. "One thing has nothing to do with the other. She just wants to be sure you're coming to Ireland with us for Christmas."

When Laila opened her mouth to say such a trip was impossible, Jess held up her hand. "Before you refuse, think about this. Abby, Trace and your nieces will be going. All of your friends will be there—me, Susie, Connie, Shanna, Bree and Heather. If you refuse to come, you'll be spending the holidays back here all alone with only your parents for company. Do you really want to endure an entire holiday season of their lectures about your many recent mistakes?"

Laila could envision the dreary situation Jess was describing all too clearly. She'd thought about it a hundred times since learning of the O'Briens' plan to take their grandmother back to Ireland for Christmas.

Laila had always dreamed of visiting Ireland. Anyone living around the O'Briens had heard enough tales about Dublin and the countryside to make it sound idyllic. She loved the O'Briens—one of them a little too much, as a matter of fact. The temptation to say yes was nearly overwhelming, which was why she'd spent the last month studying brochures for holiday cruises and Christmas tours of Savannah and Charleston— anything to avoid giving in and going on a trip that had emotional disaster written all over it.

"I can't," she said, proud of herself for choking out the words.

Jess actually seemed a little startled by her flat refusal. "Of course you can."

"Have you forgotten that the reason I am in this tiny little office rather than my great big impressive one at the bank is going to be in Ireland with the rest of you?"

"Matthew? Well, of course, he'll be there, but it's not about you and Matthew. It's about Gram. It's about Susie and Mack finally being able to celebrate their marriage and Susie beating cancer. Focus on all that. Hang out with the rest of us. You'll hardly have to set eyes on Matthew if you don't want to."

That, of course, was the problem. She *wanted* to set eyes on Matthew. She wanted to throw herself into his arms, drag him into the biggest, softest feather bed around and have her wicked way with him. The man was like an addiction, one she hadn't been able to kick no matter how hard she'd tried.

"Jess, you have no idea how badly I want to go with you, but I just can't. The timing is all wrong."

Her friend regarded her with a knowing expression filled with sympathy. "Because you're still in love with him, aren't you?"

"Absolutely not," Laila said emphatically. "What Matthew and I had, it had nothing to do with love."

A grin spread across Jess's face. "Who are you trying to convince, my friend? Me or yourself?"

"You, of course," Laila insisted. "I know how I feel."

"You know how you *want* to feel," Jess corrected. "But it's not working out so well for you, is it? You haven't gotten him out of your system. Not even close."

Laila wanted to deny it, but Jess was right. Since she couldn't utter an outright lie, she said, "Look, I agreed to work for the inn. Take your one victory and go."

Jess dutifully stood up, started for the door, then turned back. "You know he's miserable, don't you?" she said softly, the parting shot coming as she hesitated in the doorway. "I know my cousin has his faults. Heaven knows, he has a history of being a huge flirt, a player, whatever you want to call it, but it was different with you, Laila. It really was. And having both of you miserable when it doesn't need to be that way doesn't make a lot of sense to me."

"It's the way it has to be," Laila reiterated, unmoved. "We never should have gotten involved in the first place. The whole relationship was crazy, like some kind of fantasy. Matthew's years younger than I am. It never would have lasted. I was just a temporary infatuation for him. If I hadn't broken it off, eventually he would have. It was better this way."

"Says who?"

"I say it," Laila told her, holding her friend's gaze with a steady look.

Jess clearly didn't believe her. And Laila was having a hard time convincing herself. She knew, though, that she had to. It was the only way she'd ever be able to move on with her life.

"So help me, Matthew O'Brien, if you don't make things right with Laila, I will never forgive you," Susie declared, standing over her brother's desk and glowering at him.

Matthew glowered right back. "Not at work, Susie," he warned. "We're not discussing my personal life here. I mean it."

Naturally, she ignored him. "I will not have this honeymoon trip ruined, to say nothing of how terrible Gram will feel if you're moping around Ireland missing Laila."

"I won't mope. I promise."

She merely scowled at the offer. He sighed.

"Isn't it enough for you that you have a clean bill of health from the doctor, and that your marriage to Mack is solid?" Matthew asked her plaintively. "Do you really need to meddle in my life, too?"

"Actually this isn't about you. It's about me and my happiness. I want Gram's trip to Ireland to be perfect, and it won't be if the entire family—the entire *extended* family—isn't there."

He pushed aside the architectural rendering he was

supposed to have finished days ago. Lately his concentration was shot. He met his sister's gaze.

"Look, nobody wants Laila in Ireland more than I do," he admitted. "I'd planned to ask her to marry me there on Christmas Eve, if you'll recall. That's no longer in the cards, obviously, since she won't even speak to me. If I try to talk her into going, she'll turn me down flat. If her presence is so critical, put somebody else on the case."

"I've already sent Jess," Susie admitted. "No luck."

"What about Trace? Surely her brother can talk some sense into her."

"She's not speaking to him at all. She's lumped him in with her parents. They're all the enemy right now. She wouldn't even return Abby's calls, and those were about work. She's cut herself off from practically everyone." She regarded him earnestly. "I'm worried about her, Matthew. If you really care about her, you should be, too."

Matthew groaned, knowing he was at least in part responsible for Laila's isolation. "How did this turn into such a huge mess?"

Susie didn't hesitate. "Because the two of you kept everyone in the dark about your relationship," she said readily, always eager to enumerate his many flaws as she saw them. "You snuck around town for who knows how long like a couple of criminals. It left everyone to conclude that even you knew that your dating was somehow wrong. It made it seem as if this were just another stupid fling for you and that Laila was ashamed of being another one of your conquests. If you'd been open about it in the first place—"

"I wanted things out in the open," he snapped. "Laila thought it was a bad idea. Seems to me she was right. The minute her stodgy parents got wind of what was going on, all hell broke loose."

"Whatever," Susie said, not one bit swayed by truth or logic. "You're the only one who can get through to her now. Apologize, grovel, beg, heap on a boatload of guilt about how the trip won't be the same without her, whatever you need to do. Just don't take no for an answer. You have to get her to come to Ireland. You got her into your bed, which, given how sensible she usually is, had to take some smooth talking. Surely you can convince her to go on a family vacation."

"The only way I'm likely to pull it off would be to tell her I'm staying home," he said realistically.

"Not an option," Susie declared. "Find another way. I mean it, Matthew. You love her. She loves you. This standoff has to end." She leveled a look into his eyes. "I expect you to handle it. Do *not* let me down."

With that she flounced out of his office. He stared after her, wondering when she'd turned into such a demanding woman, sure of her convictions. It probably had a lot to do with the grit and determination she'd found to fight ovarian cancer, to survive it against all odds. Nothing much scared her anymore, certainly not her brother.

A few months ago he'd have said he shared his sister's intrepid, determined nature. In the face of Laila's uncompromising rejection, in the wake of her stubborn stance that they were destined to ruin each other's lives, he was no longer half so sure of himself. He'd thought they could weather the fallout from people finding out about their relationship, but they hadn't. Laila hadn't even wanted to try. She'd barely stuck it out a few weeks before calling it quits.

He'd found her attitude annoying, insulting and demeaning. It trivialized what they had, in his opinion. What he hadn't been able to figure out was why he loved her anyway.

Still, he had his pride. Groveling, apologizing, begging, all those things his sister had recommended were out of the question. He'd put his heart on the line. He'd made his case. More than once, in fact. If that hadn't been enough, then why would he go back for more ego bashing?

Besides, being in Ireland with Laila, knowing that he'd intended to make it the most romantic holiday of their lives, that he'd planned to propose to her there on Christmas Eve…it would be torture, and he was no masochist. This was Susie's trip. If she wanted Laila along, then she was going to have to find some way to convince her to go.

And if she did? Well, he'd worry about that only if Susie managed to pull off some sort of holiday miracle.

"Well?" Nell O'Brien demanded as she sat in her cozy kitchen with two of her precious granddaughters. The Irish-breakfast tea was strong, the blueberry scones fresh from the oven.

She'd sent Jess and Susie on a personal mission to straighten out this ridiculous standoff between Matthew and Laila, but it was obvious from their troubled expressions that they'd failed.

"Laila refuses to go," Jess admitted. "I know she wants to, but she's as stubborn as any O'Brien."

"As for my brother," Susie said, "he's actually hurt that she dumped him. As badly as he wants Laila in Ireland with the rest of us, he refuses to do a thing to make sure she goes." She shook her head. "Men and their stupid pride! Heaven save us."

Nell knew exactly what she meant. Her grandchildren had inherited many fine qualities from their parents and from her, but stubbornness wasn't among them. Unfortunately, they all had it in spades. She supposed it was handy in certain situations, gave them the stick-to-it strength and resolve to weather many tough crises, but most of the time it interfered with their happiness. They'd be far better off with a little more tolerance and a little less bullheadedness.

"Do the two of you have any ideas?" she asked. "I will not have this family trip ruined because we're all thinking about the one person who isn't there."

"I don't think Laila views herself as indispensable," Jess said. "Or as a member of the family. She's pretty down on herself and her own judgment these days. And she's not overly fond of anything O'Brien, either."

"She's down on herself because she fell in love with Matthew?" Nell asked incredulously. "Nonsense! I'll admit to having a few reservations when I first heard about those two, but she was good for him. Anyone could see that."

She thought about her grandson and the changes she'd seen in him after he'd gotten involved with Laila. "She steadied him, made him want to settle down. I think it worked the other way around, as well. Her life needed a little shaking up after growing up with stuffy old Lawrence Riley for a father and trying to meet his old-fashioned expectations. Just his reaction to her relationship with a fine man like Matthew speaks for itself about how out of touch he is. Matthew put some color in her cheeks and a sparkle in her eyes. Lawrence should have been singing his praises for that, not condemning the two of them."

She gave her granddaughters a bewildered look. "What kind of man doesn't put his own daughter's happiness first?"

"I don't think Mr. Riley thinks much beyond what's good for the bank," Jess said. "Look how he coerced Trace into working there, even though anyone could see how miserable he was. He loves being a graphic designer. Thank goodness, he was able to get back to that."

"Well, it's about time Mr. Riley thinks about what's good for Laila," Susie said vehemently. "And there's no question that my brother was very good for her. The first time I saw them together, once I got over the shock, I realized how perfect they were for each other. They complemented each other, just as you said, Gram. Matthew couldn't keep his eyes off her, and Laila looked like a teenager. She couldn't stop blushing." She paused reflectively. "Of course, maybe that had something to do with the wine I kept pushing on her to get her to open up and tell me what was going on."

Jess nodded slowly. "So we all agree that Mr. Riley is the real problem here, right?"

"Looks that way to me," Susie said.

"Okay, then," Jess said. "Do you suppose if Laila's

father changed his mind, maybe gave them his blessing, it would help?"

Nell shook her head. "That would be like getting a tiger to change his stripes. Lawrence has never admitted to a mistake in his life. He's all but publicly disowned Laila now. He's not going to back down."

"Maybe Mrs. Riley," Susie began, but again Nell shook her head.

"She's a lovely woman, but she's always done exactly what her husband expected of her," Nell said.

"Then you could talk to him," Jess suggested. "He'd listen to you. Or maybe Dad."

"I don't think we want Mick in the middle of this," Nell said quickly. "His meddling generally backfires. Even though things work out eventually, it's usually in spite of your father, not because of him."

"I agree with that," Susie said. "Uncle Mick's well-intentioned, but involving him is a bad idea. Surely you can see that, Jess."

"Hey, I'm willing to look at any and all options," Jess argued. "Don't dismiss Dad just because he drove us a little crazy. He's one of the few people in town with more power than Lawrence Riley. People respect him, even Mr. Riley. I'll bet Dad could turn this whole situation around if he said a few words to the right people, persuaded them to talk to Mr. Riley."

"True," Nell said. "But I think this situation calls for more finesse than Mick, bless him, possesses. I suppose it's up to me."

Both of her granddaughters looked relieved.

"What are you going to do?" Susie asked, her eyes

alight with curiosity. "Something sneaky and devious, right?"

Nell gave her a chiding look. "Sneaky and devious are not traits I condone," she scolded.

Both young women simply laughed. Nell shrugged.

"Well. Not ordinarily," she said sheepishly. After all, it was pointless to fib when everyone knew she had as many matchmaking tricks up her sleeve as anyone else in the family.

"What's it going to be, Gram?" Jess prodded.

"I'll have to give that some thought," Nell murmured, then looked from one beloved granddaughter to the other. "But this O'Brien holiday of ours is going to wind up with someone walking down the aisle, no matter what I have to do to make sure that happens."

2

Laila stood beside the window in her new office at The Inn at Eagle Point and watched the whitecaps on the Chesapeake Bay roll toward shore. She'd only been here a few days, but she knew she'd never tire of that view.

"Sis?"

She whirled around at the sound of Trace's voice, a scowl in place to greet him. "What do you want?"

"We need to talk," he said firmly, already stepping into the office and closing the door behind him.

"I can't imagine what we could possibly have to discuss. You made your opinion of my relationship with Matthew quite clear. Then you got Mom and Dad all stirred up to boot." She regarded him accusingly. "We both know how that turned out."

"I'm sorry," he said simply. "I never expected things to get so far out of hand. I was worried about you, and I thought they had a right to know." He looked chagrined. "I should have anticipated that Dad would get on his high horse and say something that would force your hand."

"Yes, you should have."

"Still, quitting was pretty rash and impulsive, Laila."

"Here we go," she muttered.

"Okay, I'm lecturing," he admitted. "But don't you think you should reconsider leaving your job? Maybe try to make peace with Dad? For as far back as I can remember, all you wanted was a chance to take over at the bank for Dad one day."

"Well, it's never going to happen," she said wearily. "I've accepted that. You're not going to be able to intervene and make it right this time, Trace. Dad obviously doesn't want me there. He never did, and I handed him the perfect excuse to make it official."

"He didn't fire you," Trace reminded her. "You quit."

"Oh, please," she protested. "That's little more than a technicality, under these circumstances. The handwriting was on the wall. You didn't hear him. He treated me as if I didn't have a brain in my head, as if my going out with Matthew was the next worse thing to stealing the life savings of little old ladies. What choice did I have? Sooner or later I was going to have to stand up for myself with him. If it hadn't been over this, something else would have come along."

Trace continued to look dismayed. "Laila, be reasonable. That's in the past. You're no longer with Matthew. I have that right, don't I? Just tell Dad that. It would make all the difference."

She frowned at him. "Come on, Trace. None of this is really about me and Matthew. Dad wants the prodigal son in that job, not me."

"That ship has sailed," her brother said fiercely. "Dad knows that."

She smiled. "You don't really believe that, do you? How many times since I left has he called you with some crisis only you can resolve? Compare that with the fact that he hasn't once reached out to me, not personally, not professionally."

Trace gave her a rueful look. "Okay, you're right. He hasn't given up entirely on luring me back, but that doesn't mean I'm going to do it. You were meant for that job, Laila. You and I both know that. So does Dad, when he's not being impossible."

She couldn't deny the truth of that. Ironically, her instinct for numbers, accounting and banking had been honed at her father's knee, for all the good it had done her. Maybe it was because she had a real aptitude for it. Maybe it was simply because she'd craved his attention and approval. Look where that had gotten her, she thought wryly.

"Yes, I was perfect for it," she conceded. "But as far as Dad's concerned, I'll never be more than second best. I'm not willing to accept that. I've moved on. I'm not beating my head against that particular wall ever again. I can make a good living with accounting."

"It's not about earning a decent wage," Trace argued. "It's about doing what you love, what you were destined to do. Don't settle, Laila."

"I'm not settling. I'm accepting the inevitable. If I'd done that years ago, my life would have been far less frustrating."

Trace frowned. "You're sure about this?"

"A hundred percent," she said with what she hoped sounded like total conviction.

"If you say so," he said skeptically. "And it really is over with Matthew?"

"It really is. You can rest easy. Your sister is no longer interested in disgracing the family name."

Her response seemed to make him unhappy. "It wasn't about me or the family name," he said with obvious frustration. "How could you even think that? I just didn't want Matthew messing with your head."

"Well, he's not messing with any part of me now. You should be thrilled."

He winced. "You'll find the right guy," he said, seeking to reassure her. "I could ask Abby—"

"Don't you dare!" she ordered, horrified. "I do not want your wife parading a bunch of men in front of me."

"It was just a thought," he said defensively. "I feel as if it's my fault you're miserable."

"I'm *not* miserable," she insisted. "I'm in transition." She was pleased with the word. It described exactly where she was in her life, somewhere between the happiness she'd never expected and the uncertain future that was somewhere around the corner.

Trace stood up, apparently satisfied. "We're good, then?"

She sighed and crossed the room. For all of his annoying flaws, he was a good brother. One of the best. "Of course we're good," she said, hugging him fiercely. "Just try to remember you're a Riley, not an O'Brien. Meddling doesn't come naturally to you. You made a real mess of it this time."

"Again, very, very sorry," he said contritely, a twinkle back in his eyes. At her skeptical look, he said, "Okay, at least a little bit sorry. I think you can do way better than Matthew."

"You probably ought to leave before I feel compelled to argue with you about that," she responded.

"Love you."

"You, too," she said, watching as he left.

From the window moments later, she could see him crossing the inn's lawn and heading down to the beach to walk along the shore to the home he'd bought for himself, Abby and his twin stepdaughters. He was whistling, obviously pleased that the visit with Laila had been a success, that their relationship had been mended, if not hers with their father.

She shook her head. She knew her brother loved her, knew he wanted her to be happy, but he didn't have even the tiniest bit of insight about what it would take to make that happen. If he had, he'd have understood that her best chance at happiness was with the man of whom he'd so vocally disapproved. Not that she intended to admit such a thing to Trace or anyone else. She could barely even admit it to herself.

After a frustrating hour of holiday shopping when her heart hadn't been in it, Laila was eating a solitary evening meal at Sally's when she looked up to see Nell O'Brien standing beside her table. The place was jampacked with other shoppers, holiday carols were being played on the sound systems here and in every store in town, which had left Laila somehow feeling more alone and out of sorts than ever. She'd barely touched her meal, which by now was cold and unappetizing.

"May I?" Nell asked, gesturing toward the empty seat across from Laila. "I swear I'm just about worn out from Christmas shopping, and I've barely gotten started."

"Of course. Have a seat," Laila said. "Tell me why on earth you're shopping here, when you'll be spending the holidays in Dublin?"

"Oh, you know how it is," Nell responded after ordering a cup of tea and a bowl of Sally's homemade vegetable beef soup. "There are a lot of people who'll be expecting a little something. Many of them no longer have family around, so it's up to friends like me to make sure they aren't forgotten."

"Wouldn't they be happier with a gift from Ireland?" Laila inquired.

Nell chuckled. "Oh, they'll be hoping for that, too, if only a small token so they'll know I was thinking of them. I suspect I'll be coming back with a lot of soft woolen scarves that'll be perfect for the chilly Chesapeake Shores winter."

Laila hesitated. She was the one who'd brought up Ireland, but she wasn't really sure it was a topic they ought to be discussing. The whole subject was fraught with peril, especially for her. Still, there was little point in pretending the big family vacation wasn't just a couple of weeks away.

"You must be getting really excited about the trip," she said, treading carefully. She hoped Nell couldn't see through the casual indifference she was trying to project. "How long has it been since you've been back?"

Nell's expression turned nostalgic. "The last time was the year before my husband died, so quite a while.

I'm anxious to visit one last time, to see the few friends who are left, and to show some of my favorite spots to all the grandchildren and great-grandchildren. I want them to understand where their family came from. I might not have grown up in Ireland the way my ancestors did, but it's in my blood and my descendants'. I knew that the first time I set foot on Irish soil."

"I know Jess is looking forward to it," Laila said. "It was practically all she talked about the last time we spoke." Of course, the real focus had been on getting Laila to come along, but that was best left unsaid.

"I think she and Susie are almost as excited as I am," Nell agreed. "There's nothing quite like Ireland at Christmas, you know. There are so many decorations. The holly is especially bountiful over there. Windows are lit with candles to welcome neighbors." Her eyes filled with delight. "There are just so many wonderful traditions I've missed. My parents tried to keep some of them alive here, but it's not the same. I didn't realize that until I'd gone to live with my grandfather for a year. Summer visits were one thing, but being there for all the seasons, and especially Christmas, was magical."

"I wish…" Laila began, then cut herself off with a shake of her head.

Nell's expression brightened. "Wish what, my dear? That you could be there? You should be. We'd love for you to come. You're very much a part of this family."

Laila sighed. "Not really."

"You're Trace's sister, aren't you? And Abby's sister-in-law? You've been in and out of Mick's house and mine practically since you could walk. In my book, that makes you one of us."

Laila noticed that she'd made no mention of Laila's past relationship with Matthew. Even Nell obviously understood it had been little more than a passing infatuation.

"Jess told me I'd be welcome, but I'd feel out of place," Laila admitted.

"Not because of Matthew, I hope," Nell said. "No one is holding that against you."

Laila bristled at her choice of words. "Against me?" she repeated. "I know O'Briens stick together, but why would anyone hold what happened against me?"

"Well, you did dump him, after all," Nell said, her tone matter-of-fact. "Family loyalty surely puts us on his side, though I know you must have had your reasons. Still, all of us understand that the relationship simply wasn't meant to be. There are no hard feelings."

Laila knew she should bite her tongue, but she couldn't let the comment go unchallenged. "No offense, but Matthew has some responsibility for what happened. He's not exactly a saint."

Nell chuckled. "Not exactly," she said agreeably. "Much as I love him, I would never suggest such a thing."

"Then why do I get the feeling that you're heaping all the blame for what happened on me?"

Nell regarded her innocently. "Is that the way it sounded? I didn't mean for it to. I know as well as anyone how impossible my grandson can be. I'm sure he must have done something perfectly outrageous for a kind, considerate woman like you to drop him the way you did."

"There was no dropping," Laila insisted stiffly. "It

was a mutual decision." More or less, anyway. She'd said there was no way they could continue to see each other, and he'd gone along with it. She'd hated that almost as much as she'd hated her father's disdainful, unyielding attitude and the rift that had created.

Nell looked surprised. "Is that so? Matthew certainly seemed to suggest… Well, never mind. I must have gotten it wrong."

Laila frowned. "Exactly what did Matthew say?"

"That he was paying the price for your father's ridiculous stance, that on some level you still want to get back into your father's good graces and that cutting Matthew out of your life was the first step." She shrugged. "I can understand how he might have come to that conclusion. Your father's not an easy man, now, is he?"

"No, he's not, but the whole idea that I broke up with Matthew to appease my father is insane," Laila said indignantly. "I'm not even speaking to my father, much less trying to win him over. He has nothing to do with this. I'm done trying to jump through hoops to please him."

"I hope that's true," Nell said gently. "You're a smart, thoughtful woman, Laila. You should be deciding things for yourself, especially when it comes to choosing the man you'll love."

"And that's exactly what I did," Laila said heatedly. "I decided Matthew was all wrong for me. He agreed."

"If you say so," Nell murmured. She seemed to be fighting a smile.

Laila couldn't believe that Matthew was going around town psychoanalyzing her. Wasn't that Will

Lincoln's domain? Jess's husband was the shrink in the family.

"I have to go," Laila said abruptly. She stood up, pulled a twenty from her purse and left it on the table. Though she felt like storming out, good manners had her bending down to kiss Nell's cheek. None of this was her fault, and she was only expressing whatever nonsense Matthew had fed her. "If I don't see you before the trip, I really do hope you have a wonderful time."

"Happy Christmas to you, too, dear," Nell responded.

Happy? Laila couldn't imagine anything less likely, but at the moment she wasn't concerned with holiday spirit. No, what mattered to her right now was straightening out the infuriating and apparently very chatty Matthew O'Brien before he managed to turn the whole town against her.

The last person Matthew expected to find on his doorstep on a frigid December night was Laila. She was shivering, either from the cold or indignation. Judging from the sparks flashing in her eyes when he opened the door, it was probably the latter.

"How dare you!" she said as she walked right past him, took off her coat and tossed it in the general direction of a chair. It missed, but she left it where it had landed.

When she whirled to face him, her eyes were blazing. He hadn't seen that much heat in them since the last time they'd made love. In full fury like this, she reminded him of some kind of mythical goddess—statuesque, strong and wildly desirable. He jammed his hands into his pockets so he wouldn't reach for her.

"Something I can do for you?" he inquired mildly. "You look upset."

"I just had a fascinating conversation with your grandmother," she announced. "It seems she, and probably everyone else in town by now, is under the impression that I dumped you, that poor Matthew did nothing to deserve such a thing."

"You did dump me," he replied reasonably.

"We agreed," she insisted, her agitated pacing starting to make him a little dizzy.

He shook his head. "Sorry to contradict you, sweetheart, but you said it was over, tossed me out of your apartment and told me never to darken your door again."

She frowned, probably annoyed by his depiction of what had happened.

"It was hardly that dramatic," she said.

"Pretty much," he insisted, amused despite himself that she'd somehow turned herself into the victim here.

"But you agreed we were over," she countered.

"No, I said it was pointless to try to argue with you when you were being irrational. Then you slammed the door in my face."

"Well, of course I did," she retorted. "Who wants to be accused of being irrational by some condescending man? And just so you know, I am never irrational. I thought the whole thing through and came to a sensible conclusion."

"Not from my perspective, but you certainly did sound convinced about what you were saying. It's little wonder I took you at your word and stayed away."

She looked taken aback by his response, as if she'd never considered that, by avoiding her, he was only doing as she asked. "You never took me at my word before."

At the surprising hint of wistfulness in her voice, he regarded her with confusion. "You wanted me to fight you, to keep coming back even though you'd told me rather plainly not to?"

She sighed and sat on the edge of the sofa, her expression a little lost. The hint of vulnerability made his gut twist.

"I sound totally ridiculous, don't I?" she said. "I'm not a woman who doesn't know her own mind. At least I never was until I got involved with you. You confuse the daylights out of me, Matthew, and, to be perfectly honest, I don't much like it."

He sat a safe distance away from her to avoid the temptation to take advantage of all the mixed signals she was sending. Pulling her into his arms would be exactly the wrong thing to do. Sex wasn't the answer, not this time. Sex between them might be mind-boggling, but it wouldn't solve their problems. If he wanted her back in his life, he had to find another way.

"Understandable," he said quietly. "You're a woman who likes being in control."

She gave him a startled look, as if she hadn't expected him to get that. Then an even deeper sigh shuddered through her. "I've missed you," she admitted. "I've hated not seeing you, not talking to you."

"The lack of sex?" he inquired.

She gave him a wry look. "Yes, that, too, Matthew."

"Well, if you came over here tonight for some kind of booty call, you're out of luck," he told her. "I don't do that anymore."

She regarded him with disbelief. "Since when?"

"Since I grew up, matured, whatever you want to call it." He grinned at her. "See, you've ruined me for other women. And, just so you know, I'm not sure I'm crazy about that, either."

She sat in silence for a while, then regarded him with a helpless expression, or at least as helpless as a woman with her boatload of strength was ever likely to display. "What happens now, Matthew? I still think I was right to walk away. So many things happened. I lost so much. I already blamed you for that. I figured over time the resentment would only grow and destroy us. I figured it was better to cut our losses."

Here was the opening he'd been waiting for. "Do you honestly want to know what I think?"

"Of course."

"I think you panicked and ran because we'd moved way past your comfort zone. As long as you thought it was just about sex, you were fine, but then you threw away your job at the bank. That terrified you, because you'd never expected anything or anyone to matter more to you than that job. I obviously did, and it scared you."

She blinked at his assessment, but she didn't even try to deny it. "Have you been talking to Will? You sound way too much like a shrink."

"Hey, I've been known to have an insight or two all on my own," he protested. "But, yes, Will did share a few observations. So have Jess, Susie, Uncle Mick and just about everyone else in the family. We've been the talk of the entire O'Brien clan for a while now. Frankly, it's getting a little tiresome. I wish my brother would go back to dating my brother-in-law's ex-lover so they would focus on somebody else for a change."

Momentarily distracted, Laila regarded him with shock. "You don't really think Luke and Kristen belong together, do you? That's just crazy."

"Good grief, no. That's what makes it so perfect. The family would be freaking out about it, and we'd be off the hot seat. We could figure things out without all that well-meaning interference."

An oddly hopeful expression crossed her face. "Maybe then I could go to Ireland and wouldn't feel as if we were under a microscope every second," she said, then winced. "Sorry. Forget I said that. I can't possibly go to Ireland. It would send entirely the wrong message."

Despite her quick retraction, Matthew's heart took an unexpected lurch at the mention of the family trip. He had no idea what had really brought her over here tonight, but he couldn't blow this tiny opening with some careless remark.

"Why not? You're as much a part of this family as anyone. Everyone would love for you to be there. Frankly, I've been taking a lot of heat because you decided against going. You'd be doing me a favor, not that you owe me anything," he added quickly.

"Hardly," she said, regarding him with amusement.

"I'm just saying you should go." He hesitated, then admitted, "I already have your ticket, as a matter of fact."

Her mouth gaped. "You bought a ticket for me?"

"Months ago," he confirmed. "No refund, so it'll just go to waste if you don't change your mind. I know how much you hate throwing money away. It's practically your obligation to go."

"I could just pay you for the ticket, then use it some other time," she countered, though there was an undeniable spark of excitement in her eyes.

"And pay all those charges for changing it? Not very frugal," he chided.

"What about a hotel room? Did you think about that? I'm sure everything's booked by now."

"I booked a room for us, but I can bunk in with Luke, if you'd prefer that. It's not a problem."

"Really? You'd do that?"

"I told you I'm not just after your body. I'm willing to make a few sacrifices to prove that to you."

She actually looked a little disappointed by that news. "You do still want me, though, right?"

Matthew couldn't help it. He laughed. "You are a very contradictory woman."

"That doesn't answer the question."

"I could prove how much I still want you in half a second, Laila, but I'm not going to," he said, his tone a whole lot more noble than the desire thrumming through him. "If we start over, and I'm sensing that might be a possibility here, then we're going about it the right way this time. No more extremely hot, middle-of-the-night trysts."

"You mean no sex?" She seemed a little shaken by that.

"No sex," he confirmed, barely able to choke out the words.

"What'll we do?" she asked, sounding bewildered.

"Now, that's just downright insulting," he said indignantly. "We've been known to have intellectually challenging conversations."

"Sure, in bed," she replied, then grinned. "But maybe we could compromise."

He was fascinated by the suggestion. "Compromise how?"

"We could talk *first*."

Though Matthew laughed at her notion of compromise, he refused to back down. "Nope, I think we'll do this my way. You'll come to Ireland. I'll share my brother's room. And I'll court you like the fascinating lady you are in full view of my family."

"I'm not all that enamored with being a lady," she complained. "That's why being with you was such a refreshing change. You saw me in a completely different light, as an unpredictable woman who was impossible to resist. I liked that."

"Oh, if you must know, you're still plenty tough to resist, but I'm going to pull it off." He looked her over with just enough heat in his gaze to make his point. "Those are the terms. Are you in or out?"

"Your grandmother says there's no place quite like Ireland at Christmas," she said wistfully.

"Is that a yes?"

She took a deep breath, met his gaze, held it for what felt like an eternity, then finally nodded. "Yes, I'll go with you."

Matthew resisted the desire to get up and do a little jig. There'd be plenty of opportunities for that once they got to Dublin.

Laila gave him a wry look. "You do know we just got manipulated by a master, don't you?"

He regarded her blankly. "Who? How?"

"Your grandmother, of course. I didn't see it at the time, but every word she said to me at Sally's tonight was calculated to get me to race over here and confront you." She shook her head. "I thought I was smarter than that."

Matthew gave her a consoling look. "Don't feel bad. We've all been taken in by Gram a time or two."

This time, though, he was going to owe his grandmother big-time for accomplishing what no one else had been able to. She'd broken the impasse between him and Laila. Now it was up to him to make sure the détente turned into something that would last.

3

Laila arrived in Dublin with the first wave of O'Briens. The rest—Thomas and Connie, Jake and Bree, Connor and Heather, Kevin and Shanna—weren't arriving for a few more days. There were so many of them that Mick had chartered a bus to take them to the hotel after the overnight flight.

Somehow Laila had ended up seated next to Matthew, who turned out to be a surprisingly adept tour guide. He pointed out all the sights and offered one amusing anecdote after another as they rode toward St. Stephen's Green and their hotel in the heart of downtown Dublin.

When she managed to tear her gaze away from the ornate, colorful doorways decorated with lush holly wreaths and the window boxes overflowing with ivy, evergreens and bright flowers, she turned to find him regarding her with amusement.

"What?" she demanded.

"You're as excited as a kid on Christmas morning."

"You've been here before. I haven't. It's everything I imagined it would be."

He smiled at that. "Glad you came?"

She ignored the last of her reservations about being here in such close proximity to him. "Very glad," she said, unable to tear her gaze away from his.

He attempted a frown. "Now, don't be looking at me like that, with your eyes all sparkly and dreamy."

She nearly laughed at his suddenly solemn expression. "Why is that?"

"You'll be giving me ideas, and I've made a promise to you to keep my hands to myself. It's nearly impossible when you look at me like that. I'm a mere mortal, and no mortal man can be ignoring the invitation I'm seeing in your eyes."

For a moment Laila had forgotten all about the promise, all about her own resolve to make this trip about Nell's happiness and Susie's, about sightseeing and enjoying a new holiday experience, and not about Matthew and her thoroughly confusing feelings about him. Now all of that ripped through her, leaving her with a whole passel of conflicting emotions.

"Good point," she replied, trying to match his solemn tone. "I'll have to watch myself." She quickly looked out the window again. "Now, where are we exactly?"

Matthew leaned closer to peer out the window, deliberately crowding her, if she wasn't mistaken. He grinned when she scowled at him.

"Lost my head," he claimed, moving back before pointing out various highlights of the shopping along Grafton Street.

At the hotel, rooms were quickly assigned, luggage deposited. Left alone, Laila gazed with regret at the huge comfortable bed and its fluffy down comforter. It was going to be very lonely, especially knowing that she could have been sharing it with Matthew.

When there was a tap on the door, she threw it open, relieved to have her train of thought interrupted. Unfortunately, though, it was Matthew himself in the hallway.

"I thought you might be too excited to be taking a nap," he said. "How about breakfast and then a walk through the neighborhood? Who knows when the sun will be shining brightly like this again? We should take advantage of it, and that should tire you out so you can catch a couple of hours of sleep before the family festivities get into full swing late this afternoon. Uncle Mick's taken over an entire pub for tonight, I think. He believes we should start as we intend to finish—with Irish music, a hearty meal and a few pints of Guinness."

Laila hesitated, then shrugged. She knew sleep was out of the question, and Matthew's company on a busy street was no more dangerous than lying alone in that decadent bed thinking about him and wishing he were there with her.

"Give me two minutes to freshen up," she said, hurrying to wash her face, run a brush through her hair and spritz herself with a light fragrance she knew Matthew liked.

When she walked back into the bedroom, she looked down at her clothes and frowned. "This outfit looks as if it's been slept in, which it has. I should change."

"You look fine," he assured her. "If you look too perfect, I'll be fighting off men on every corner."

She laughed. "Now, there's the O'Brien blarney in full force. Come on. I'm starving."

To her surprise, they were the only members of the family in the hotel dining room.

"I thought for sure some of the others would be down here," she said, glancing around.

"You worried about being alone with me, sweet-heart?"

"Hardly," she fibbed. "I just assumed everybody else would be too excited to settle down right away, too, especially Carrie and Caitlyn. They were bouncing up and down with energy on the bus to the hotel."

"Oh, believe me, those two were so hyped up after the flight that Trace and Abby immediately headed to the park across the street so they could run wild." He studied her. "Would you feel better if we joined them?"

Laila considered the offer for a split second. "No way," she replied. "The food's here."

She ordered a pot of tea, a bowl of steel-cut oatmeal with fresh berries, along with scrambled eggs and toast. She studied the menu warily. "Do I want to try some of these more traditional things?"

Matthew chuckled. "Probably not on the first day," he advised, then ordered the same things she had.

After they'd ordered and the waiter had brought their tea, she sat back and looked around the hotel dining room. It could have been any hotel anywhere in the world, but it was Dublin! And, risky though it was, she was here with Matthew!

"I can't believe I'm really here," she said happily.

"Are you glad you changed your mind about coming?"

"Yes. I would have hated to miss this."

He leaned forward as if he had something more to say, only to see Luke appear, pull out a chair and join them. "You don't mind, do you?" he asked, though he was already seated.

Matthew frowned at his younger brother. "I thought you were going to rest or go for a run or something."

"I ran. I showered. And now I'm ready for a full Irish breakfast," he said, looking around for their waiter.

"Did it even occur to you that you might be interrupting?" Matthew asked testily.

Luke gave him an innocent look. "Interrupting what? The way you explained it to me, you two are adhering to a hands-off policy while in Ireland, which is why you're in my room instead of Laila's."

Laila nearly choked on a sip of tea. She frowned at Matthew. "You told him that?"

"Well, I had to explain why I needed to bunk with him, didn't I?"

"He did," Luke concurred. "Because I was hoping to get lucky on this trip and now my plans for a thoroughly raucous holiday are seriously thwarted."

Laila studied Luke's expression and thought she detected a hint of sadness behind the cavalier attitude. "You aren't seriously missing Kristen Lewis, are you? I thought that was over, or that it was some kind of ploy to keep her away from Mack, whatever."

"Kristen and I had fun, no question about it," Luke said. "But that's all it was."

Laila heard the false note in his voice and shook her head. "Not buying it. It might have started out that way, but something changed. You fell for her, didn't you?"

Matthew regarded her with surprise. "You can't be serious. Luke and Kristen? It was a fling." He turned to Luke. "Right, bro?"

"Sort of like you and Laila," Luke retorted, then glanced apologetically toward Laila. "No offense."

"None taken," she said. "Why didn't you ask Kristen to come along on this trip if you're really hung up on her?"

"And have Susie string me up by the you-know-what?" Luke said with a shudder. "No, thank you. She's not entirely over the fact that Kristen was once Mack's lover, even though it was years and years ago. I don't think she's anywhere near ready to welcome her into the family fold."

Laila was impressed that he was sensitive to that. "How about you? Does it bother you that Kristen and Mack had a thing?"

Luke shrugged. "Everybody has a past, and I know Mack and Susie have something really special going. It's not an issue."

Matthew rolled his eyes. "Delusional," he muttered under his breath.

Luke's gaze narrowed. "Meaning?"

"Mack's feelings aren't really the problem, are they? You should be worrying about the fact that Kristen still has feelings for him. Isn't that the reason you set yourself up to provide a distraction in the first place, to keep her away from Mack?"

For a moment Luke looked taken aback. "Okay, sure," he said eventually. "But everybody's moving on now." His voice didn't hold much certainty.

Matthew just shook his head.

Laila gave Luke's hand a squeeze. "Be careful, okay? Sometimes it's very difficult to get over an old flame, even when you know it's the only thing to do."

"Which explains why you and my brother are sitting here having a cozy breakfast together, instead of sitting all alone in your separate rooms?" Luke taunted.

"Watch it," Matthew warned.

Laila, however, laughed. "Out of the mouths of babes," she murmured. "Yes, Luke, walking away from Matthew has been much harder than I expected." She gave Matthew a defiant look. "But I will pull it off eventually."

There was no mistaking the sudden twinkle in Matthew's eyes. "I look forward to seeing you try," he said mildly.

"You might not want to turn this into a challenge," she warned him. "I can match you stubborn streak for stubborn streak."

Matthew winced. "Good point."

Fortunately their breakfast arrived just then, which gave them both time to retreat from positions that might have proved indefensible. While Matthew sulked and she fretted, Luke dug into his food as if he didn't have a care in the world. Laila scowled at him.

"He is annoying," she commented, as if Matthew had just recently mentioned it.

Matthew glanced at his brother. "Very annoying."

Luke merely chuckled. "See, though, I've brought the two of you into agreement over one thing. It's a fine start for the first day of the trip."

Nell stood across from Trinity College in downtown Dublin and stared at the window of the tobacco shop that had once belonged to her grandfather. She knew that once she walked through that door, it would be like going back in time. That was one reason she'd never chanced it on previous trips. Some things were better left in the past. Charles would never have understood about those long-ago summers before they'd married.

She'd spent so many afternoons in the shop during the summers her parents had sent her here to stay with her grandparents. Surrounded by the rich scents, she'd sip tea and pretend to read books as she listened to her grandfather talk to his regular customers. They said women were gossips, but she learned more about what was going on in the city right there in that room than she ever had by reading a newspaper or a history book.

Of course, her fear of crossing the shop's threshold was about more than that.

"Gram, don't you want to go inside?" Susie asked, slipping an arm around her waist.

"I'm not sure I want to know if there have been too many changes," she admitted. "Dillon O'Malley, who bought it from my grandfather, is surely retired by now. I don't know how it will feel to find a complete stranger behind the counter." Nor did she know how she would feel if she happened to be wrong about that and, instead, came face-to-face with Dillon for the first time in all these years.

"I could at least go in and ask who owns it now," Susie offered. "Then you could decide."

Nell seized on the suggestion. "Would you mind?"

"Of course not," Susie said, giving her grandmother's hand a reassuring squeeze before heading inside.

Nell all but held her breath as she waited for Susie's

return. "Well?" she asked, searching her granddaughter's face for answers when she came back.

"The man I spoke to says he's Dillon O'Malley."

Just as Susie spoke, the man himself appeared in the doorway, his eyes filled with curiosity. Tall, with only the barest stoop to his broad shoulders and just a hint of silver in his black hair, it was unmistakably Dillon. When his gaze settled on Nell, he seemed to go perfectly still.

"Nell?" That one word was part confusion and disbelief, part hope.

Nell reached out to Susie to steady herself as she looked into the clear blue eyes of the man she'd once been so certain she was meant to marry.

"Hello, Dillon," she said softly.

He shook his head. "After all these years I'd have known you anywhere," he said. "You're as beautiful as ever with your red hair and those grand eyes."

She laughed. "And you're as full of blarney. My hair hasn't been red in years. I can barely find a few strands amid the gray to remind me of the shade it once was."

"In my eyes, you're the lass you were the last time I saw you," he insisted.

For just an instant, Nell allowed herself to feel like that girl again, young and carefree and wildly in love for the first time in her life. She'd been Nell Flanagan then.

"Come in, Nell," Dillon pleaded. "Talk to me. Tell me about your life." He glanced again at Susie. "This has to be your granddaughter."

"She is. Just one of them. This is Susie O'Brien Franklin."

Dillon clasped Susie's hand, though his gaze remained locked on Nell. "And she brought you to Ireland for the holidays? What a lovely thing to do."

"Actually this is her honeymoon trip," Nell said wryly. "Can you imagine? She insisted that the whole family accompany her."

Dillon laughed. "Then she is, indeed, truly a Flanagan with a huge heart. I look forward to getting to know you, Susie."

"So, you and my grandmother go way back?" Susie asked, her face alight with curiosity.

"Way back," Dillon confirmed.

"Did she always have a wild and reckless streak?" Susie asked.

He laughed. "You have no idea."

"Stop it, you two," Nell ordered. "I've never been wild or reckless."

"You went back to America and broke my heart, did you not?" Dillon asked.

Nell frowned at him. "I'm quite sure there were plenty of women around to mend it. Christina Ahearn comes to mind. Didn't you marry her not long after I'd gone home that last time?"

"Only after I was convinced you were never coming back," he insisted. "Now, come inside. I'll brew some tea. I have the Earl Grey you love so much."

Nell stared at him in amazement. "You remember that?"

He held her gaze. "I remember everything," he said solemnly.

Susie regarded them hesitantly. "Should I leave you two to catch up?" she asked.

Nell hesitated, torn. She wanted to know everything

about Dillon's life, wanted to fill in all the blanks that her grandparents had been so careful to leave unanswered once she'd gone.

Yet so many years had passed. What was the point at this late date?

Still, when she looked into Dillon's hopeful eyes, she couldn't say no. "I'd love tea," she said at last, then squeezed Susie's hand. "I'll be fine here for an hour. Why don't you come back then?"

"Or I could see that she gets back to her hotel," Dillon offered.

"I'll come back," Susie said, apparently sensing that Nell needed backup. She smiled at them. "Enjoy your visit."

Dillon escorted Nell inside, waited as she looked around.

"You've kept it mostly the same," Nell commented.

"How could I change a thing, when everywhere I looked I saw you?"

She shook her head. "You shouldn't say things like that."

"Why not, if they're true?"

"You're married to someone else," she reminded him.

"Christina died ten years ago," he said, then held her gaze. "And your husband?"

"Gone, too," she said softly.

"Then there's no reason for us to feel guilty for indulging in a bit of nostalgia, is there?" he suggested. "Come in the back and I'll make that tea. There's a lot of ground to cover and you've only given us an hour to do it." He studied her. "Or will you be in Ireland for a while?"

"Two weeks," she admitted.

His expression brightened. "Then there's time for a nice, long visit. This will just be the first of many, I hope."

Nell couldn't argue. She hoped so, too. After all these years, her heart had taken a little leap at the sight of this dear old friend. It was too late to go back in time. She wouldn't want that, anyway. But to have a few days to recapture those old emotions, to experience just for a moment that surge of optimism that came with spending time with a man who appreciated her, well, she wasn't going to deny herself that.

Mick frowned as Susie sat in the lounge with him, Megan and Jeff describing the meeting between his mother and Dillon O'Malley.

"You think there's some kind of history there?" Mick demanded irritably.

"It looked that way to me," Susie said. "Neither one of them explained anything more than that they'd known each other years ago, but there were definite sparks in the air. Who knew that Gram had a secret past?"

"It's not something to brag about, if she does," Mick said testily.

"How do you know a thing like that?" Jeff asked reasonably.

"Has she ever mentioned Dillon O'Malley?" Mick responded, then answered his own question. "No, she hasn't. And do you know why? Because she's ashamed of it, I'll guarantee you that. I need to take care of this."

"Let it go, Mick," Megan commanded. "You're not

rushing over there to intrude on their reunion or to rescue your mother."

"Well, who knows what sort of man this Dillon O'Malley is? For all we know he's gotten wind of the fact that the O'Briens are well-to-do and he plans to take advantage of Ma."

His brother frowned at him. "And how would he know a thing like that?" Jeff asked. "Would he have stored away this knowledge just in case the entire family decided to pay a visit to Dublin one day? You're acting crazy, Mick. Didn't Susie just say that Ma didn't even know if he was still running the store our great-grandparents once owned? Obviously they haven't kept in touch."

Mick regarded his brother accusingly. "Don't tell me you don't worry about Ma."

"I worry about Ma falling and breaking her hip," Jeff countered. "I worry about her feeling lonely in that little cottage of hers. I don't worry about her finding a companion whose company she enjoys."

"Then you're naive," Mick grumbled.

Megan rested a hand on his arm. "Nell is a wise woman, Mick. She'll see right through anyone trying to take advantage of her."

"Of course she will," Susie said adamantly. "I only told you because I thought it was sweet, not so you'd get all worked up. Now I'd better walk back over there to get her. I told her I'd be back in an hour."

"I'm coming with you," Mick said, standing.

"No, you're staying right here with me," Megan countered. "You are not going over there and embarrassing Nell in front of an old friend."

"Well, someone who doesn't have all these stars in their eyes ought to check things out," he argued. "Susie's besotted by love these days."

"I still have my brain, Uncle Mick," Susie retorted patiently. "If something doesn't seem right, I'll handle it. And if you're really worried, I'll ask Mack to come with me. He could probably take Dillon O'Malley in a fight, though the man looked pretty fit for his age."

"Taking Mack along is probably a good idea," Mick said, looking relieved.

Susie rolled her eyes. "I was joking."

"Well, I'm not. What if Ma gets some crazy idea about inviting this man to join us tonight? Are you going to put a stop to that?"

"Absolutely not," Megan said firmly. "And if she does, you'll welcome him and be on your best behavior."

Mick shook his head. He should have known he'd get no help from the rest of the family. They all lived in a dream world. It was up to him to keep an eye on things. That was his role in this family, and he took it seriously.

He watched Susie leave, then said casually, "I think I'll take a walk."

"No!" Megan and Jeff said in chorus.

Defeated, Mick sighed.

Megan patted his hand. "Let's go up to the room. Maybe I'll be able to think of some way to distract you."

Mick regarded her skeptically. "How?"

Jeff clapped his hands over his ears. "Megan, please do not answer that till I'm gone," he pleaded.

After he'd left, Mick turned to Megan, intrigued despite himself. "You were about to say?"

"I think I'll let my actions speak for themselves,"

she taunted, standing up and beckoning to him. "You interested?"

He grinned at his wife, happy to see the lively spark of passion in her eyes. "You don't have to ask me twice."

She laughed. "Good. For a minute there, you had me worried."

"Ah, Meggie, you never have to worry about a thing like that. You'll fascinate me till the day I die."

She linked her arm through his and led the way to the elevator. The promise in her eyes made all his cares fade away. There'd be time enough later to worry about what his mother was getting herself into with this O'Malley fellow. And whatever it was, he'd fix it.

4

Matthew was very glad he'd paid attention to everything he'd been told by his family on prior trips to Ireland. His running commentary as he took Laila on a walking tour of the bustling streets around the hotel seemed to be relaxing her. She didn't even object when he tucked her arm through his and kept her close by his side. For a couple of days she'd managed to elude him by going shopping with his cousins, but today he'd found her alone and managed to lure her away from the hotel.

"Look at these window boxes," she exclaimed time and again, pausing to take pictures of the colorful flowers mixed with holiday greenery. "People need to do this in Chesapeake Shores. See how cheerful it makes everything look?"

"Winters are milder here," Matthew reminded her. "Not by a lot, but enough to make a difference. And I think everyone's a little obsessed with flowers to counteract the dreary weather. We actually have plenty of sunshine in Chesapeake Shores."

She looked momentarily deflated, but then her expression brightened. "Do you think you could make window boxes for my apartment?"

"Me?"

"You're an architect. Design something."

He chuckled. "Window boxes weren't exactly part of the curriculum in architecture school."

"Mick probably never thought he'd be creating a flower shop work space for Bree, but he pulled it off," she challenged. "The way I hear it, you're as good an architect as your uncle is."

He regarded her with amusement. "Is that a challenge?"

She laughed. "Pretty much. Maybe we could even have a design competition, get everybody in town involved. I'll have to warn Jake and Bree, since it could be big business for his nursery and her flower shop. We could turn Chesapeake Shores into the flower show-place of the Eastern Seaboard."

"You never think small, do you?"

"No," she said readily. "How about you?" Her expression turned serious. "Are you happy designing houses like the one you did for Susie and Mack? Or do you want to take on a whole community someday, the way Mick has done?"

He hesitated, unsure what her reaction was likely to be, then admitted, "Actually I'm designing a community in Florida right now."

She stopped and faced him, her eyes alight. "You are? Why didn't I know that?"

"It's not as if we've had a lot of conversations recently. A developer contacted Mick a couple of months ago. Mick had me sit in on the meetings, then told me to take charge of the project. He's overseeing my work, but it will be my vision."

"Matthew, that's amazing!" Suddenly the light in her eyes dimmed. "Tell me about it. Are you designing just the houses or everything?"

"Everything, from the single-family homes and town houses to the retail area, from the town green to the pedestrian-only streets, even an elementary school," he said, unable to contain his pride over the confidence Mick obviously had in him. With that confidence came a huge burden of responsibility. Mick's reputation would be on the line, along with his own.

"Does that mean you'll be spending a lot of time in Florida?" Laila asked.

He nodded. "At the time it didn't seem like much of a drawback, but now I have to wonder...." His voice trailed off. If they were to get back on track, did he dare spend so much time away from home right now?

"You have to do it," she said staunchly. "Matthew, it's an incredible opportunity, and Mick is showing a tremendous amount of faith in you. You can't let him down."

"But you and I, we've barely begun to reconnect." He searched her face. "Or don't you see it the same way? Are we starting over or not?"

"I'm not entirely sure what we're doing," she responded candidly. "This is a vacation. It's not a real test of anything. Whatever we do, we have to move forward slowly this time. We rushed into a relationship before we thought it through before. Maybe having you working out of town will be exactly what we need so we don't get carried away and do something impulsive. The distance might give us the perspective we need to decide whether we really do belong together."

He couldn't help smiling. "I thought you liked the impulsive streak I bring out in you. At least that's what you've always said."

"True," she admitted. "But it's not really me."

"Which was exactly the point, I thought. You said you liked stretching your boundaries."

"Maybe I stretched them a little too far. I was way beyond my comfort zone when we were together. Accountants and bankers, we don't take a lot of risks. We're known for our caution and sensible decisions."

"I don't think you went too far," he said solemnly, looking into her eyes, then brushing a curl from her cheek. "Maybe you were out of your comfort zone, but I love the impulsive, unpredictable you."

"But not the staid, ordinary me?" she asked, sounding resigned. "See what I mean? We're too different, Matthew."

"Hey, there is nothing staid or ordinary about you," he protested. "Not even on your worst day. You can be thoroughly responsible when it comes to work and still have a wild side, Laila. You're a complicated, complex woman. Don't put yourself into some tiny niche and be afraid to expand your horizons. Then your father wins."

"I don't know," she said, though she looked hopeful.

He waved off the entire conversation. It had gotten way too serious. "Enough about the future and enough self-analysis," he said. "I see a pub just ahead and it's calling our names."

She regarded him with amusement. "Really? I don't hear anything."

"Then you obviously haven't been in Dublin quite long enough."

"Will I be seeing leprechauns soon, too?"

"After enough Guinness, it's entirely possible," he told her, leading the way into the pub, which had a fire burning in the hearth and a jovial lunch crowd of local workers and holiday shoppers crammed into every corner.

He spotted a pair of empty seats, squeezed through the throng to order two pints of ale, then wove his way back to find Laila laughing with a couple of young Irishmen at the next table. His heart stumbled at the sight, but he managed to keep his own smile in place as he joined her.

"These handsome brothers claim to be O'Briens, as well," Laila told him. "Should I believe them?"

Matthew regarded them skeptically. "Sounds a bit convenient to me, though few men would make such a claim without proof."

"And we have it right here," one said, drawing out a photo ID, which, sure enough, was for Sean O'Brien.

The other did the same, and his name was Liam O'Brien. "Could it be we're distantly related?" he asked Matthew. "I've been wanting to go to the States. Having a few relatives to take me in would prove handy."

"You've been wanting to go to California to be in films, Liam," his brother reminded him. "These folks are from the other side of the country. Obviously those geography classes we took in school were wasted, if you don't know the difference. Not that it matters, because you'll not be going and you'll not be in films. Your skill's with numbers and keeping books, not acting."

Laila regarded the unfortunate Liam with sympathy. "I'd like to do something wildly creative myself, but my skill, too, is with numbers. I'm an accountant, as well."

"Now, what are the odds of such a thing?" Liam asked, obviously delighted by the coincidence. "It's bloody boring, isn't it?"

"Bloody boring," Laila confirmed.

"Laila, however, is anything but boring," Matthew felt compelled to state.

"Goes without saying," Liam said sagely. His brother, Sean, nodded agreement.

"Thank you," Laila said.

"Will we see you again, beautiful Laila?" Sean inquired.

"Not bloody likely," Matthew murmured under his breath, not sure why he was so annoyed by their harmless flirting. Maybe it was because Laila seemed so pleased with it. Maybe it hadn't been wise to encourage her reckless side, if this was how she intended to behave.

"You should come by the hotel and meet Nell," she said. "That's Matthew's grandmother. She'd know if your families are linked. We'll introduce you, won't we, Matthew?"

He bit back a groan. "I'm sure Gram would be happy to meet you both," he said with undisguised reluctance.

They made arrangements to stop by at the end of the day, then left. When they were gone, Matthew turned to

Laila. "What was that about? I leave the table for five minutes and you pick up two men?"

"I didn't pick up anyone," she said, frowning. "They were just being friendly. Then we discovered the coincidence of their being O'Briens."

"For all we know they have a dozen different photo IDs to suit the name of any American tourist anxious to explore their Irish roots. They could be practiced con men."

Laila gave him a chiding look. "You sound as cynical as Mick. You heard him go on and on at dinner the other night about Nell's old friend, as if Dillon O'Malley were out to steal her blind."

"Well, Uncle Mick has a point. You can't be too careful these days," Matthew grumbled, knowing he was starting to sound ridiculously paranoid. Better that, though, than have her see his behavior for what it was, pure jealousy.

Laila studied him intently. "You're not worried those two charming rogues are going to take advantage of the O'Briens," she accused. "You're jealous."

He winced at the direct hit. "I was hoping you wouldn't pick up on that," he admitted.

She grinned. "How about that? Another first in my life. I've actually made a man jealous."

"You don't have to sound so darn proud of yourself."

Laila chuckled. "Actually, I do. I'm beginning to think if I stick with you, I could discover all sorts of fascinating new sides of myself. Perhaps I was too hasty in cutting you entirely out of my life."

"And will you delight in driving me a little crazy in the process of all this self-discovery?"

She patted his cheek. "Just a bonus, I assure you."

Matthew sighed. He'd actually caught a few glimpses of hope this afternoon that they were inching back onto the right track. He just hoped he survived long enough to make it to the finish line.

"Matthew was actually jealous because I was having a perfectly innocent conversation with a couple of men in a pub," Laila exulted over tea with Connie and Jess later that afternoon. Connie and Thomas had arrived earlier in the day, and the women had immediately gone off on an outing. "Can you imagine? I've never made a man jealous before in my life."

Connie chuckled, but Jess didn't look nearly as pleased. "Do you really want to test Matthew's patience? Isn't your relationship complicated enough without throwing strangers into the mix?"

"Oh, for goodness sakes, he knows I'm not interested in those men. Talk about the ultimate in geographically undesirable. They live in Dublin, remember."

"People have been known to relocate for love," Connie pointed out. "Just look at Thomas. He's actually commuting to Annapolis from Chesapeake Shores these days. I offered to move, but he says our real roots are in Chesapeake Shores and that my job with Jake requires me to be out too early to be driving any distance. Wasn't that considerate of him?"

Both Jess and Laila chuckled at her thoroughly besotted expression.

"We all know he'd do whatever it takes to keep you very, very happy," Jess teased. "He's so grateful that a much younger woman would take him on."

"As if he's the lucky one!" Connie scoffed. "He gets a rebellious teenager in the bargain. Jenny's not adapting all that well to having a stepfather. Those two dance around each other like a couple of sparring partners, and I hold my breath waiting to see who's going to land the first blow. Poor Thomas. He had no idea what he was letting himself in for. He's so unsure what role he should be playing that I think he's just about bitten through his tongue to keep from saying the wrong thing."

Laila frowned. "It's not causing problems for you two, is it?"

"Absolutely not," Connie said. "I won't allow my daughter to ruin this. We're going to work it out like the mature, rational adults at least some of us are."

Laila regarded her intently. "How's Sam reacted to having Thomas in the mix? Is he suddenly feeling territorial about his daughter?"

"Jenny has barely been a blip on Sam's radar since her birth," Connie said bitterly. "He's probably relieved that he doesn't even have to pretend to care anymore. I think that's part of the problem. Thomas *does* care, but Jenny doesn't trust it at all. She's so used to being ignored, she figures Thomas is only attentive to her to try to score points with me."

"Uncle Thomas will get through to her eventually," Jess said. "He's so good with all the nieces and nephews. I always thought it was a shame he didn't have kids of his own."

Laila grinned. "So, how about it, Connie? Any talk of that?"

Connie looked nonplussed by the question. "A baby? Me and Thomas? Do you two recall how old I am?"

"You're not too old," Laila insisted.

"You don't think so?" Connie asked, sounding intrigued. "We haven't really talked about it, at least not much. Thomas mentioned it, but I'm not sure he was serious. I told him the same thing, that I'm too old to even consider such a thing."

"Maybe you should reconsider," Jess suggested. "Laila's absolutely right. You're not too old now, but there's not a lot of wiggle room here. Another couple of years and that ship will have sailed. Think about it while it's still feasible."

"A baby," Connie repeated. "You really think it's not too late?" Suddenly she sounded a little awed by the possibility.

Laila and Jess exchanged a look. The seed was duly planted, Laila thought, congratulating herself.

Jess glanced around the table. "Isn't it pathetic that we had to come all the way to Ireland to find enough time to have the kind of gabfest we used to have all the time back home?"

"I've missed these," Laila said. "Now that you two are settled, it's much harder to find girl time."

"Well, we're going to do it," Jess declared. "A few minutes at Sunday dinners in the middle of that mob scene just aren't enough."

"Agreed," Connie declared. "Laila?"

"Count me in. Something tells me I'm going to need a lot of advice in the coming months, especially if Matthew is spending most of his time in Florida."

Jess and Connie both looked taken aback.

"Florida? Why would he be in Florida?" Jess asked.

"Your father's assigned him to a new community development project down there," Laila said. "You didn't know?"

"Dad hasn't said a word," Jess said.

"And Thomas is the last to get filled in on family gossip," Connie added. She studied Laila worriedly. "How do you feel about this? When did you find out?"

"Just today," Laila told them. "And I'm not sure how I feel. Maybe it's for the best. We certainly won't be doing anything rash, will we? Having some space probably makes sense."

"But you hate it," Jess concluded. "You don't want space. Why don't you tell Matthew that?"

"How can I? This is an incredible opportunity."

"It is," Connie agreed. "But that doesn't mean you have to like it. At least let him know you'll be miserable without him."

"Maybe I won't be," Laila suggested hopefully.

"In what universe?" Jess scoffed. "You've been miserable when he's only been blocks away. I say it's time to stop hesitating and grab what you want. Why are you even in separate rooms on this trip? It's not as if anyone would be shocked or appalled if you shared a room."

"Nell might be," Laila said.

Jess laughed. "Are you kidding? I think she'd be so relieved to have the two of you finally showing some sense, she'd do a little dance outside your door."

Laila frowned. "She's a little more old-fashioned than that, I'm sure."

"Well, she might bring a priest and a special marriage license along with her," Jess conceded. "But that wouldn't be such a bad thing, either."

Laila held up her hands. "Hold on! It is way too

soon to be talking about marriage. Just a few days ago I wasn't sure we should even be dating."

"Well, I'm not sure about that, either," Jess retorted. "I think you should just go for it and stop analyzing everything to death. You know you're perfect together."

"We're perfect together in bed," Laila corrected. "The rest hasn't been tested all that thoroughly."

"Unless you're talking pharmaceuticals and maybe airplanes, testing might be overrated," Connie suggested. "I'm with Jess. Go for it."

"You two are just blinded by your rose-colored glasses," Laila said. "I'm trying to take a mature, clear-eyed view of things."

"Boring!" Jess declared.

If she'd accused Laila of anything else, it might not have had an effect, but these days Laila was very sensitive to any suggestion that she was boring.

"I'll give it some thought," she told them as she scooped an extra helping of Devon cream onto her scone. She'd discovered it was almost as satisfying as rocky road ice cream.

"Overthinking, testing, it's all part of the same cycle of deliberation," Connie noted. "I'm with Jess. Sometimes you just have to go for broke. Follow your bliss, isn't that what they say?" She grinned. "And being with Matthew is pretty blissful, isn't that right?"

Laila ignored the deliberate taunt. "Could I point out that neither of you exactly rushed headlong into a relationship, much less marriage?" she said testily.

Jess grinned. "And look at all the time we wasted. You should learn from our mistakes and jump straight into marriage. Do not second-guess yourself, Laila."

Sadly, Laila realized she was far more tempted by the idea than any sane woman ought to be. And for the past hour, she'd only been drinking strong black tea, so she couldn't even blame overindulgence in Guinness for making her a little crazy.

Matthew nearly lost it when he spotted Laila in the hotel bar with Sean, Liam and Gram. The men were clearly making a fuss over both women, charming them with who knew what kind of smooth talk. He saw red just thinking about it.

He crossed the lobby in long strides, walked into the bar and managed to make room for himself on a sofa between Sean and Laila, who regarded him with unmistakable amusement. For that matter, Gram seemed to be highly entertained by the obviousness of his behavior, as well.

"So, are these long-lost relations of ours?" he asked, his skepticism plain.

"It could be that we have a distant uncle in common," Gram said. "I never knew all of your grandfather's relatives, so the O'Briens are a bit of a mystery to me. Liam has promised to bring their family Bible by tomorrow, so we can look through it together."

"Isn't that great?" Laila said.

"Yeah, great," Matthew said without enthusiasm. "Gram, don't you want to rest before dinner?"

"I had a nap earlier," she said. "And Mick's promised an early night. We're just going up the street for a bite to eat, which I've translated to mean that once again I'm not to invite Dillon O'Malley to join us." She rolled her eyes. "As if I'd pay a bit of attention to Mick if I wanted Dillon there."

"How is Mr. O'Malley?" Laila asked in a teasing tone.

"Every bit as charming as I remembered," Nell said, a flush on her cheeks.

"Then why don't you include him tonight, if you want to? I've heard there's dancing on the agenda," Laila said.

Nell shook her head. "I believe only you young people are going out for music and dancing after dinner. I need my rest tonight. Dillon and I are taking the train to Howth tomorrow, so I can walk by the sea. I have many fond memories of that little town."

"Oh, that sounds wonderful," Laila said, her expression wistful.

"Then you must come along," Gram said at once. "Matthew, what about you?"

He wasn't about to miss a chance to spend the day with Laila, especially a day that didn't include distant possible relatives. "Sure, I'll come."

"It'll be cold by the water," Liam warned. "Be sure you dress warmly."

Nell laughed. "Oh, I'm not so old that I've forgotten how chilly it can get. I imagine we'll find a lovely place to stop for lunch, as well. Dillon seems to know exactly the sort of cozy, inviting places I like."

The two young men stood. "Well, we'll leave you to your evening, then," Sean said. "It's been a joy to meet you. I surely hope we do find some family connection." He winked at Laila. "Though I can't help thinking it's a blessing you're not an O'Brien. You're fair game for a bit of flirting."

Matthew seethed, especially when Laila didn't say a word to discourage them. Instead, she actually walked with them as they left the hotel.

After they'd gone, his grandmother regarded him with a tolerant expression. "Your green is showing," she chided. "And I'm not referring to your Irish heritage. Don't you know that those two young men mean no harm? And since you've no claim on Laila, she's done nothing wrong, either."

He sighed. "I know that."

"Let me ask you something. Do you want that young woman in your life permanently?"

Matthew started to utter the knee-jerk denial that he might have a few months ago, but he realized it was no longer true. It might never have been true, in fact. He'd been certain about what he wanted from Laila practically from the beginning of their relationship. She was the one filled with doubts. From time to time, her certainty had spilled over to shake his resolve.

"Yes," he admitted candidly.

"Then tell her that," Gram advised. "Better yet, show her."

"How?"

She smiled at him. "That engagement ring you bought isn't doing a bit of good burning a hole in your pocket. Put it where it belongs."

He shook his head. "She's not ready."

"She's not, or you're not?"

"I just told you that I want to marry her. Why else would I have bought the ring?"

"Hesitation never wins a man what he wants," she advised. "You, my handsome grandson, are smart as a whip about many things. You may even have an insightful moment or two."

"Thanks, I think."

"Oh, that was fair praise," she said. "What you're not is a mind reader, not even when it's the woman you love. Don't make decisions based on what you *think* Laila wants or what you *think* she might be ready for. Act on your own desires and let her decide for herself. She could surprise you."

She glanced beyond him and smiled. "Here she comes now. I'll leave you two on your own. Don't waste another opportunity."

He stood when she did, then hugged her. "Thanks for the talk and the advice, Gram."

"Anytime. That's what I'm around for, to try to steer you young people in the direction you want to go. Sometimes it's clear you're not listening to your hearts the way you should be."

On her way past Laila, she murmured something Matthew couldn't hear, then went on toward the elevators. Laila's gaze followed her before she turned back to Matthew.

"What were you two discussing?" she asked.

"This and that," he told her. "What did she tell you?"

"That I'd never go wrong listening to my heart."

Matthew smiled. "She said pretty much the same thing to me, though you got the condensed version."

Laila smiled. "I love your grandmother."

"So do I. Now, do you really want to spend this evening with the entire family or should we sneak off and do something on our own?"

"Such as?"

"We could have dinner in your room," he suggested.

She laughed. "And we both know where that would lead. I thought you'd made a vow to keep your hands to yourself on this trip."

"Temptation keeps getting in my way," he retorted. "But if that's out of the question, let's go dancing."

"Isn't that what everyone else plans to do later?"

"Ah, but they're going someplace traditionally Irish where the dancing will be energetic. I've something a bit more romantic in mind."

She studied him a moment. "You're in an odd mood tonight."

"You can thank my grandmother for that. She's been putting ideas in my head."

"Romantic ideas?" she asked, looking startled.

He nodded. "Does that scare you?"

She held his gaze, her cheeks tinted pink with a surprising blush. "Not half as much as it should."

"Then we have a date?"

"We have a date," she said solemnly.

"I'll let the family know," he said. "Grab your coat and meet me back here in ten minutes."

She started toward the elevators, then turned back. "Matthew?"

"Yes?"

"We've never had a real date before."

"Of course we have," he said, then paused and thought about it. "We really haven't, have we?"

What they'd had were occasional drinks that had

led to bed, a quick meal that had led to bed, a heated glance across a room that had led to bed. They had spent an awful lot of time with their clothes off and practically none out in public being a couple, discussing each other's hopes and dreams.

He smiled at her. "We're way overdue, don't you think?"

"I don't know. It's recently been suggested to me that dating is highly overrated."

"Who on earth said that?"

"Jess and Connie."

He laughed. "Well, just look who you were talking to. Those two did everything humanly possible to drag out the entire dating process because they were terrified of making a commitment. Now that they have, they have the enthusiasm of the recently converted. I think we owe it to ourselves to give dating a chance."

Laila nodded, then gave him a heated look that just about melted his resolve.

"As long as it doesn't take too long," she said, her gaze pointed. "I've been thinking that maybe I'd like to be a convert, too."

For the first time in weeks, maybe months, Matthew's heart soared. Maybe Gram was right and he'd been misreading all the signals. Maybe what he wanted was right in front of him, if only he'd reach for it.

5

Nell thought she detected a flare of disappointment in Dillon's eyes when she arrived at the train station with Matthew and Laila in tow.

"Dillon, this is my grandson, Matthew O'Brien, and his friend, Laila Riley. Her brother, Trace, is married to my granddaughter Abby."

Whatever his disappointment, Dillon was too much the gentleman to make the young people feel uncomfortable. He gave them a beaming smile and took their hands. "It's a pleasure to meet more of Nell's family, though I admit I've been wondering why I've yet to see the first sign of her sons."

"Mick and Jeff have been busy, and Thomas, in fact, has just arrived," Nell was quick to say.

"As if that has anything to do with it," Matthew teased. "Believe it or not, my grandmother is afraid my uncle Mick might forbid her to see you. He seems to have a real aversion to the idea of her dating."

Dillon chuckled until he looked into Nell's eyes. Then he reacted with dismay. "Can this be true? Your son disapproves of your dating, even though you've been a widow for some time now?"

"He's simply having a little difficulty getting used to the idea," Nell said, scowling at Matthew for making such a revelation. "For now I'm trying to be considerate of his feelings. You'll all meet when the time is right."

"Which, if Gram has her way, will be on the day we leave for home," Matthew countered, a twinkle in his eyes. "I think she enjoys sneaking around and making my uncle a little crazy."

Nell scowled at him. "Young man, you are not too old for me to send you back to the hotel to your room."

Matthew laughed. "Will you send Laila with me?"

"She's done nothing wrong," Nell pointed out. "And that would turn a punishment into a reward, now, wouldn't it?"

"To say nothing of the fact that I intend to see Howth today," Laila added. "Matthew, behave yourself. Stop teasing your grandmother."

Matthew sighed dramatically. "Now you've taken all the fun out of the day."

Dillon looped an arm around his shoulders. "Buck up, Matthew. You've a beautiful woman by your side and we're going to a picturesque seaside town. If you can't enjoy yourself under those circumstances, then you're not any relation of Nell's. She's a woman who's always been able to find joy in any moment."

Nell regarded Dillon with surprise. Was that how he remembered her? All she recalled were the tears she'd shed when she'd finally made her choice to leave Ireland and return to Maryland and the life her parents had wanted for her with Charles O'Brien. Duty had trumped what she'd felt at the time, convincing her it couldn't possibly be anything more than infatuation. She'd left so much misery in her wake. All she remembered of that time was the heavy burden of her guilt. Time, apparently, had washed away whatever bitterness Dillon must have felt back then.

She saw the sign on the platform flash, indicating that their train was arriving. Her heart skipped a beat at the prospect of a day's adventure down memory lane. This time, she assured herself, they would be happy memories. She'd make sure of that. How could they be otherwise when she was surrounded by people she loved?

"This hands-off business is good for us, don't you agree?" Laila asked as she and Matthew followed the winding stone walkway that led along the edge of the sea at Howth. It curved around to create a charming marina that reminded her of Harbor Lights back home.

They'd left Nell and Dillon in a cozy café sipping tea and eating scones. When Laila and Matthew had gone off on their own to explore, Nell had been complaining that the scones weren't nearly as good as her own.

Now, with the sea splashing against the rocks and a brisk wind blowing, Laila was chilled through, but she'd never been happier. The sun was playing tag with heavy, dark clouds and mostly winning, at least for the moment.

"You look half-frozen," Matthew noted. "Are you sure you don't want to go back and have a cup of tea?"

"Soon," she said. "Right now I just want to absorb the fact that I'm here in this lovely place."

"With me?" he asked quietly.

She turned to face him. "With you," she agreed solemnly. "That's what I meant before. I think we're seeing each other differently, now that ripping each other's clothes off isn't an option."

He smiled at that. "Is that so? How do you see me now?"

"As a wonderfully mature, complicated man who adores his grandmother," she said, then tilted her head thoughtfully. "And maybe adores me."

Heat flashed in his eyes. "I do adore you." His expression turned serious. "I love you, Laila. For months now, I've made no secret of that."

The words settled into a secret room in her heart and warmed her, but still she said, "I'm not sure I'm ready to believe that yet."

He looked puzzled. "What do you mean? You think I'm lying?"

"Of course not," she said at once. "But if I believe you, if I accept that your feelings really do run that deep, then there will be decisions to be made, won't there? I'm not ready to face those decisions. Just being with you has cost me a lot. I have to deal with that, Matthew. Otherwise, I'll wind up resenting you, which wouldn't be fair at all. That's why I called things off before."

"Do you really not know your own heart?" he asked. "Or is it that you don't trust mine?"

"A little of both," she admitted candidly, hating the hurt she saw in his eyes. "But that's why this time is so precious, Matthew. We've taken the pressure off. There's nothing that has to be decided today or tomorrow or even the next day. We're just here together." She regarded him hopefully. "Can't that be enough for you for now?"

"For now," he conceded eventually, then added earnestly, "But I want more, Laila. I want it all—the house, the family, the future. I won't settle for less, and I won't wait forever."

She frowned at what sounded a lot like an ultimatum. "It's not entirely up to you, you know."

"Believe me, I get that. You've made all the rules up to now. If you ask me, some of them haven't worked out so well, especially the one that kept our families in the dark. Maybe it's time I made a few rules of my own."

She regarded him with a narrowed gaze. "Such as?"

"Not letting you treat this relationship as if it's something to be ashamed of, for one thing. Surely, around my family at least, we can be open about it. They've done nothing but accept us as a couple."

"Agreed," she said at once. "Hiding it from them was a mistake, no question about it."

"Okay, then. And we won't let your father dictate what happens between us."

She regarded Matthew with annoyance. "I thought I'd made it clear that my father's not involved in my decisions any longer."

He tucked a finger under her chin and forced her to meet his gaze. "I know you want to believe that, want to stick to it, but his opinion still matters to you. I just want you to commit to not letting it be the deciding factor."

Sadly, she could see his reasoning. Much as she

wanted to believe she could turn her back on her father, it was going to be harder than she'd anticipated. She'd spent too many years trying to please him to change overnight.

"Fair enough," she told Matthew, pleased that he understood her so well, even if the insight didn't speak highly of her and the influence her father continued to have over her life. She either had to break that bond—sever it with no regrets, which seemed unlikely—or find a new strategy for dealing with not only her father, but her mother as well. Those two had acted as one as far back as Laila could remember, even when she and Trace had thought for sure that their mother sympathized with them.

Laila shivered once more in the cold, damp air, and this time she couldn't ignore it. "I think I'd like to have that tea now," she told Matthew.

"Good idea, since your lips are turning blue," he teased. "I could remedy that right here."

Her breath caught. "Oh?"

His gaze searched hers. "With your permission."

She nodded, unable to squeeze a single word past the lump in her throat. She wanted to be kissed here in this beautiful place, capping a memory she knew would last a lifetime.

Slowly he lowered his mouth to hers. The heat was instantaneous. It spread through her from head to toe like a wildfire burning free.

But all that heat was dangerous, she reminded herself. If she wasn't careful, she could get burned. She could lose her heart, lose the future that had once mattered so much to her.

Those thoughts snapped her back to reality. She'd already lost that future. Hadn't she been saying for weeks now that there was no going back, not to the bank, not under her father's thumb? Was she as uncertain about that as Matthew had implied only moments earlier?

Matthew, however, was here, holding her ever so gently, claiming her with a passion she'd only dared to dream of. Had she been crazy to let this go?

Or was it crazy to believe it could last?

Since she had no answer, she gently extricated herself from his embrace, pretended not to see the confusion in his eyes.

"That was nice, but I still want tea," she said, an unmistakable hitch in her voice.

Matthew looked as if he had plenty he wanted to say, but in the end, he only nodded. "Then tea it is."

"And one of those fantastic scones with lots and lots of Devon cream."

He laughed then. "Are you sure you're not Irish?"

"Sorry, no," she said. "Unless it's very distantly." She only aspired to be…by becoming an O'Brien. The thought startled her so badly, she nearly stumbled on the path and tumbled into the sea.

Matthew, of course, steadied her. "Something wrong?" he asked.

"Not a thing," she responded cheerfully. "Nothing that a steaming cup of tea won't cure."

But even as she said it, she knew it wasn't true. Only giving in to her feelings for Matthew was going to cure what ailed her. She just didn't know if she dared risk it.

* * *

Matthew had been cornered by his sister and Mack the minute they returned from the trip to Howth.

"We need your help," Susie told him, dragging him into the bar and ordering Irish coffees all around before Matthew could even speak up to say he'd prefer something a little less lethal.

"Okay, what's this about?" he asked, looking from his sister to his brother-in-law.

Mack shrugged. "Ask Susie. She's the one who has some kind of bee in her bonnet."

Susie gave him a chiding look. "Quaint expression," she commented. "I just have a few concerns. I think it's my sisterly duty to discuss them with you."

"Concerns about…?" Matthew asked, even though he had a feeling he wasn't going to like the answers.

"You and Laila. Or, rather, your intentions toward Laila. We all did our part to make sure she came along on this trip, hoping that the two of you would mend fences and get your relationship back on track." She studied him with a narrowed gaze. "I hope that wasn't a mistake."

"Why would you think it might have been a mistake?" Matthew asked.

"I'm not seeing any signs of progress," Susie said, sounding miffed.

"You're not the one who has to see them, now, are you?" Matthew responded.

"Then things are better between you?" she inquired hopefully.

He didn't even attempt to hide his amusement at this sisterly concern run amok. "I'm satisfied."

She seemed taken aback by his declaration. "Really? Seriously?"

"Yes, Suze. Things are progressing quite nicely, and I expect them to continue to progress. I assume I can trust you to leave the situation to me."

His sister looked disappointed. "You don't want my help?"

"Not so much," he said dryly.

"Good luck with that," Mack murmured.

Susie scowled at her husband. "I can mind my own business."

Both men laughed.

"In what universe?" Matthew asked.

She gave him an impatient look. "Oh, for heaven's sake, I'm just trying to help. Do you want Laila or not?"

"I want Laila," Matthew said. "But I think I'll go about winning her on my own terms, if that's all the same to you. What kind of honeymoon are the two of you having, if you have all this spare time to worry about my love life?"

"Careful," Mack warned. "I might take that the wrong way. You know perfectly well that your sister is excellent at multi-tasking, and meddling seems to be in her genes."

"Well, I'd consider it a personal favor if you'd keep your wife focused on you and out of my business." He held Mack's gaze. "Please."

With that, he stood up and walked out of the bar, but not before he heard Mack say, "I told you this was a bad idea."

Susie, to Matthew's surprise, laughed. "No, it wasn't. I found out everything I needed to know. Matthew is firmly on the hook. Now I just need to focus my energy on Laila."

Matthew groaned. He debated leaving his sister to her machinations, but he knew they'd backfire. He turned around and went back. He leaned down and looked his sister squarely in the eye. "Stay out of it, Suze," he said quietly, holding her gaze. "I mean it."

"I think he's serious, Susie," Mack commented.

"Oh, if he had any idea what was good for him, he'd have sealed this deal by now," she scoffed. "He obviously needs some help."

"Stay out of it," Matthew repeated.

She only grinned. "You don't scare me."

"Well, I should. I know your secrets. I could spread them far and wide. A few of them might even stir up this happy marriage of yours," he threatened with absolutely no intention of following through. He loved that Susie and Mack were finally together. He merely hoped to shake her up, make her think twice about messing around in his life.

"Secrets?" Mack inquired, looking from him to Susie and back again.

Susie patted his cheek. "Nothing for you to worry about," she said, then scowled at Matthew and added pointedly, "nothing!"

"Try me," he retorted, hoping the empty threat would be enough to at least slow her down, if not get her to forget her scheming.

He held her gaze steadily. She was the first to blink and look away. He heaved a relieved sigh and walked away for the second time. This time, though, only silence followed him.

* * *

Laila found half a dozen messages at the desk on her return from Howth. One was from her father. The rest were from Trace. Since her brother was less objectionable, she called him first.

"You're back?" he asked when she reached him.

"Just walked in."

"Meet me across the street in the park. We need to talk."

"I can't right now. There are some guys coming over to speak with Nell about a possible family connection, and I promised to be there."

"If you think someone should be there, Abby will go," Trace said. "This is important, Laila."

"Does this talk have anything to do with Dad calling?"

Silence greeted the question.

"You're not answering me, which can only mean yes," she said.

Trace sighed. "Then he did call you," he said, sounding frustrated. "I told him not to, that I'd talk to you."

She echoed his sigh. "What's this about, Trace?"

"He's reconsidering what happened. He wants to talk to you about coming back to work. First, though, he wants to know if it's true that you and Matthew are through."

Her brief moment of hope faded. "We're not," she said succinctly. "I imagine that changes everything."

"Just meet me and let's talk about this. I have a plan."

"Has it occurred to you that the mere necessity for having a plan to deal with Dad pretty much says how dysfunctional all of this is?"

Trace laughed. "Of course, but we're talking about Dad. It just comes with the territory. The key to success is accepting that and playing the game more skillfully than he does. Ten minutes, Laila."

"Okay, fine," she agreed.

Moments later as she walked past the bar, she noticed Matthew stalking away from a table, leaving Susie and Mack behind. He didn't look overjoyed.

"Problems?" she inquired when he exited the bar.

"Nothing that strangling my sister won't resolve," he said darkly.

"You know you don't mean that," she said.

"Well, of course I don't mean it," he said irritably. "She's just exasperating. She's all starry-eyed these days and thinks she can manipulate the rest of the world into being the same way."

"Ah, she's matchmaking," Laila concluded. "I think it's sweet."

"You wouldn't say that if you'd been there." He waved off the subject. "Never mind, I've neutralized her."

"How so?"

"I threatened to reveal all her deep, dark secrets to Mack."

Laila laughed. "Susie has no deep, dark secrets. She's the epitome of the wholesome, all-American girl."

"Of course she is, but it's made her nervous. Maybe that'll keep her in line for a while."

"Boy, are you an optimist," Laila said.

He shrugged. "Probably." He regarded her with a narrowed gaze. "Where are you going, by the way?

You're not meeting up with Gram, Sean and Liam, are you?"

"Not right now. Abby's going to fill in for me. Trace wants me to meet him across the street in the park. Apparently he's determined to mediate yet again between me and my father."

Matthew looked surprised. "Really?"

"So he says. I have my doubts that he has that much skill at mediation, but I'm willing to listen. Since a lot appears to hinge on you and me being through, I don't see this going anywhere."

"I probably shouldn't, but I find that oddly encouraging," Matthew said. "Do you want backup?"

"No, thanks. Trace isn't the problem, and my father's thousands of miles away. I've got it."

Matthew pressed a quick kiss to her cheek. "Good for you. I'll see you later. Want to walk over to the pub with me? I can stop by your room and you can tell me how things went with your brother."

"Sure."

"Then I'll see you at six."

Laila gave him a wave, then headed across the street. Just inside the park, she found a bench in the quickly fading sun. It wasn't especially warm, but she turned her face up and closed her eyes.

"You praying for patience?" Trace inquired as he sat down beside her and stretched out his legs.

"Am I going to need it?"

"We're talking about Dad, so of course," he said.

"So, what's this proposition he wants you to make to me? And what did he offer you first?"

Trace winced.

She patted his knee. "Don't feel bad. It's not your fault you're always going to be his first choice. So, what was it? Did he offer to step down as president of the bank? Give you his seat on the board? What?"

"He mentioned a few things along those lines," Trace admitted. "Frankly, I tuned him out. When he finally let me get a word in edgewise, I said no. Again. And told him he was being a stubborn idiot for not making the exact same offer to you."

"Trace, we both know that is never going to happen. Even if he begged me to come back, the most he's going to offer me is a vice presidency, and he'll do that grudgingly. He doesn't think I have what it takes to run the bank."

"You could go back, prove him wrong."

"Not if the cost of doing that is walking away from Matthew."

Trace's gaze leveled. "You told me before we left home that it was over between you. I thought you only came along on this trip so you wouldn't be alone for the holidays."

"I thought it was over." She shrugged. "Now, not so much," she admitted. "And before you get all worked up, I have no idea where this is going, but I'm not just walking away because my being with Matthew makes Dad crazy. I'm happy when I'm with him, Trace. I see myself in an entirely different way. He's good for me like that."

She regarded her brother earnestly. "Do you know what it's like to grow up with everyone around you thinking you're stuffy, reliable and boring?"

"Reliability is a good quality," Trace countered.

"But stuffy and boring aren't. Heck, I was boring myself. Remember Dave? He was perfectly suitable. Dad adored him. But even you thought I'd wind up bored to tears if I stayed with him. Matthew's taught me how to live. Really live."

"You're talking about a wild, passionate fling," Trace said. "I get that. You were probably due, but come on, Laila, you can't live your life that way. It's not realistic. Life is about compromise and being sensible, about making plans and sticking with them."

She gave him a long look. "Is your marriage to Abby that dull?"

He immediately bristled. "Of course not. We have—" He hesitated.

"Passion," she said heatedly. "That's what you have. Don't you think I can see that every time I look at the two of you? I want that, Trace. I want to feel alive when someone walks into a room and looks at me. I want my heart to pound when someone says my name. I want to see the same look in a man's eyes that you get when you see Abby, as if you're seeing the sun, the moon and the stars all wrapped up in that one person."

"And Matthew makes you feel like that?" he asked skeptically.

"Yeah, he does," she said softly. "And maybe it can't last, but for now I want it, big brother."

"Even if you wind up with your heart broken?"

She nodded, then answered with absolute certainty. "Even then."

"Okay," he said, sounding resigned. "You know all I really care about is your happiness. If Matthew can give you that and you consider it a fair trade-off for losing the career you always wanted, it's your call."

She sighed. "It shouldn't have to be a trade-off, but yes, it's worth it." It had taken her a while to realize that, but she understood it now. Life without that blood-sizzling excitement was hardly worth living.

"Shall I tell Dad that, or do you want to return his call?" Trace asked. "Maybe he'll have a change of heart if you tell him what you just told me."

She chuckled. "No, if I tell him that, what he'll have is a heart attack. You call. Tell him whatever you want to, but the bottom line is no. I won't take the job under his conditions."

And truthfully, she didn't want to risk listening to any of his persuasive arguments, especially knowing the price tag that would go along with them.

"No second thoughts?" Trace asked.

"Not a one."

"Okay, then. I'll tell Dad."

As they walked back to the hotel, Trace draped an arm around her shoulders. "I'm proud of you," he said.

She regarded him with surprise. "Why?"

"For knowing what you want and sticking to your guns. I know it's not easy. They say that Mick O'Brien is a master manipulator, but I think Dad's tactics are just as sneaky. For what it's worth, I think you made the right choice."

"You do?"

"Yep, but the first time I see you crying over Matthew, I'm going to punch his lights out."

She smiled at the fierce note in his voice. "Goes without saying," she said.

She just prayed Matthew would never give her—or her brother—any cause to make good on his threat.

6

"Have you seen Ma today?" Mick asked Thomas and Jeff when they met in the hotel bar late in the afternoon before heading out for the evening with the rest of the family.

"I heard she was taking the train to Howth and spending the day with that old friend of hers," Jeff said. "Matthew told Jo that he and Laila were going along. Surely they must be back by now." Eyes twinkling, he asked, "Did you give Ma a curfew?"

Mick regarded his brother with annoyance. "Hardly the point," he grumbled. "What is Matthew thinking by encouraging Ma to spend time with that man?"

Thomas didn't even try to hide his amusement. "You don't think Ma is perfectly capable of making her own decisions at this stage of her life? Do you know nothing of our mother? She needs encouragement from no one. She's always done exactly as she pleased."

"That's precisely what I've been telling him," Jeff

said, his gaze on his older brother. "Stir up a ruckus at your own peril, Mick. She'll spend more time with this man, if only to annoy you."

Mick frowned at the pair of them. "I have half a mind to hire a private investigator to look into this Dillon O'Malley's past. Ma would never have to know about it."

Thomas chuckled. "Have you ever known Ma to be oblivious to what's going on around her? She'll find out, Mick, and she won't be one bit happy about it. Leave it alone."

"I agree," Jeff said.

"Why am I not surprised?" Mick scoffed. "You've left *your* children to their own devices, haven't you? How long did it take Susie and Mack to finally marry?"

"They married when the time was right," Jeff countered. "No amount of interference from me would have influenced them." His expression turned thoughtful. "Mick, what is this really about? Surely you know that Ma has a good head on her shoulders. And she's more than deserving of finding a little happiness. Look at all the years she devoted to helping you raise your children. You, of all people, should want this for her."

Mick frowned. "And you'd be content if she just decided to stay here in Ireland? You don't think that would rip the heart and soul right out of this family?"

Jeff and Thomas shared a commiserating look.

"I thought so," Thomas said, sounding surprisingly understanding. "I never thought I'd see the day that something would truly rattle you, Mick, but the idea of Ma stirring up the status quo has done it, hasn't it?"

Mick knew he probably sounded ridiculous, but there

it was. He couldn't imagine life in Chesapeake Shores without Nell in the middle of things. He counted on her. She'd raised his children, for heaven's sake, just as Jeff had said. She kept the entire family grounded and, more importantly, connected. Even when he and his brothers had been seriously at odds, it was Nell's insistence that had kept them together as a family.

"Okay, yes, it scares me to think what it would be like without her," he admitted.

"She won't be with us forever," Jeff reminded him quietly. "That's the sad reality. Personally I want her to be happy for however many years she has left. If that means staying here, then I'm all for it. You know how much she's missed being in Ireland. She loved those summers she spent here with her grandparents and that entire last year before she went home to marry Dad. Don't you recall all the stories she told us? She always sounded so incredibly happy."

"So you'd let her stay, just like that?" Mick asked testily.

"It needs to be her decision," Jeff argued.

Thomas held up a hand. "Hold on, you two. We're getting way ahead of ourselves. Just because Ma is enjoying some time with an old friend doesn't mean she intends to abandon her family and stay in Ireland. We need to back off and see how this plays out." He gave Mick a hard look. "Agreed?"

"I still say we need to know more about this man," Mick countered, determined to have his way on this much, at least.

"I think you're turning this into a problem because you have too much time on your hands," Jeff retorted.

"Now that you're back with Megan and all of your children are happily married, you need something new to focus on and Ma's it."

Mick bristled at the accusation, but he honestly couldn't deny it. What he didn't understand was why his brothers weren't more concerned. He sighed heavily. Maybe, though, they were right, and there was nothing to worry about.

"Okay, I'll let it go for now," he conceded grudgingly. "But I'll be keeping an eye on things, you can be sure of that."

"Never doubted it," Thomas said.

Jeff grinned. "Happy to leave it in your capable hands."

Mick shook his head. "Why did I ever think the two of you would back me up on this?"

"I have no idea," Jeff told him.

"We haven't agreed on much in thirty years," Thomas added. "The odds were against it."

Despite his annoyance with the pair of them, Mick chuckled. "Meggie's always telling me I'm delusional. I guess she's right."

"Only about some things," Thomas consoled him. "Every now and again you show signs of pure genius."

The sincerity in his voice gave Mick pause. "You almost sound as if you mean that."

"I do," Thomas said.

"And I second it," Jeff admitted.

Mick looked from one brother to the other. "Well, I'll be. Maybe Ma's been right all these years, and we will eventually come to appreciate each other's good qualities."

Thomas laughed. "I won't press you to list mine."

"Me, either," Jeff said quickly.

Mick regarded them with unexpected warmth. "I'll work on that list and get back to you. I expect it's longer than I realized."

And for the first time in years, he thought he could see both of his brothers with clear-eyed appreciation, rather than resentment. Maybe that was one of those holiday miracles his mother was always talking about.

Laila was surprisingly nervous as she waited for Matthew to come to her room to pick her up for their romantic outing. She'd checked her makeup twice and changed her outfit three times, which was pretty much the limit since she'd brought just so many clothes along on the trip. Short of going shopping, these were her only choices.

When someone tapped on her door, she sucked in a deep, calming breath, then opened it to find Susie on her doorstep. She frowned at Matthew's sister.

"What brings you by?" she asked, not even trying to hide her suspiciousness.

"Now that's a lovely greeting," Susie said, laughing. "I thought we should have a chat, catch up a little."

Laila immediately shook her head. "Oh, no, we shouldn't. I already know you've been cross-examining Matthew. Leave me alone."

Susie grinned. "It's just an innocent conversation," she promised, slipping past Laila and heading for the overstuffed love seat by the window that looked out on the park. She patted the space next to her. "Have a seat."

"Not on your life," Laila said. "And before you start,

I am not discussing Matthew with you, period. If that's what you're here for, save your breath."

"Actually I'm here to talk about you," Susie said.

Laila knew that was only marginally better. "Oh?"

"Are you having a good time?"

No minefield there, she thought, nodding. "I am."

"I heard you and Matthew went on a day-trip with Gram and Mr. O'Malley. How was that?"

"Wonderful," Laila said cautiously. "It was a beautiful little town. The marina reminded me of Chesapeake Shores."

Susie nodded. "Sounds charming. Did you and Matthew have any alone time?"

"Describe 'alone time,'" Laila replied. "Mostly we were in public or with your grandmother and her friend."

"But you had time to talk, maybe share a kiss," Susie speculated.

Laila frowned at her. "Are you fishing or do you have some specific point you're trying to get to?"

"Just that, the way I heard it, the two of you shared a kiss that set all the hearts in Howth aflutter."

Laila tried to imagine Nell O'Brien reporting that. Or Matthew, for that matter. She couldn't. And it was doubtful that Mr. O'Malley had dropped by the hotel to fill Susie in. So, then, it had to be speculation.

Laila looked directly into Susie's eyes. "I have no idea where you could have heard such a thing."

"Then it's not true?" Susie persisted, looking a little disappointed.

Laila had a choice. She could lie through her teeth and protect their privacy, or admit the truth and deal with the fallout. Actually there was another choice: evasion. That struck her as the best of the lot.

"How's your honeymoon going, Susie? You and Mack having a good time?"

Now it was Susie's turn to frown. "I know what you're doing."

Laila laughed. "Of course you do. How about this? You stop prying into my private life and I'll stay out of yours. I know getting me to come on this trip was a personal mission for you, but it's time to stop worrying about the rest of us and focus on you and Mack. It's your honeymoon, or have you forgotten that?"

"Hardly," Susie said, her expression turning dreamy. "It's everything I imagined it would be." She grinned. "That still leaves me time to be concerned about you and my brother."

"We're adults. We can figure this out all by ourselves," Laila told her.

"Of course, but I can't help worrying," Susie said. "Matthew's crazy about you, which has to be a first for him. If you're not taking the relationship seriously, then he needs to understand that."

"I'm pretty sure Matthew knows exactly where we stand," Laila said, not even trying to hide her amusement. She'd been watching the meddling O'Briens from the sidelines for years. "You're the one who wants clarity."

"Well, of course I do," Susie said with exasperation. "He's my brother. I was an early supporter of your relationship, and then things fell apart. It broke his heart. I don't want to see that happen again."

"Neither do I," Laila assured her, relieved to hear another knock on the door. "That'll be Matthew now."

Susie's expression brightened. "You're going out?"

"We are."

"Alone." Obviously recalling her earlier mistake, Susie clarified, "I mean, without the rest of the family."

"That's the plan," Laila said as she opened the door.

Matthew was about to lean in for a kiss when he spotted his sister. "What are you up to?" he asked, his own suspicions glaringly obvious.

"Susie just dropped in for a chat," Laila said. "No need to worry. She didn't get what she came for."

"And what was that?" Matthew asked, his wary gaze still on his sister.

"The inside scoop on the status of our relationship," Laila said.

Matthew sighed. "Isn't it enough that you tried to pump me for information?" he demanded of his sister. "Did I not tell you to stay out of this?"

Susie stood up, crossed the room and gave his cheek a pat. "You involved me months ago. Don't you recall crying on my shoulder because some unnamed woman—Laila, as it turned out—had dumped you? Now I'm just doing my sisterly duty to see that it works out this time. If you don't like it, you've nobody to blame but yourself."

"It was a weak moment," he conceded. "I should have known it would come back to bite me in the butt." He gave her an earnest look. "You can stop worrying now, Suze. I've got the situation under control."

She looked vaguely disappointed, but she nodded.

"Okay, then. I'll leave you to it." She grinned. "But I will be watching, little brother. Don't mess this up."

"Not my intention," he assured her, giving her a fierce hug. "Love you."

"Love you back," she said, then turned to Laila. "You, too, by the way. I want you happy, that's all."

"And I appreciate that," Laila assured her.

After Susie had gone, Laila turned to Matthew. "We are on track, aren't we?"

"We are," he confirmed. "And getting more on track every minute." He reached for her, settled his lips over hers and kissed her until she was weak-kneed and breathless. "What do you think?"

She met his gaze, barely able to speak. "I can't think at all at the moment."

He gave a nod of satisfaction. "Exactly what I was going for. You ready for our date?"

She nodded. If she was any more ready, they'd never get out of this room.

Matthew and Laila were just finishing their decadent dessert when he gazed into her eyes and announced casually, "I think we should talk about children."

Laila choked. "I beg your pardon? Whose children? Caitlyn and Carrie? Little Mick?"

"Ours," he said calmly.

She swallowed hard. "I'm not following. Give me a minute to catch up."

Matthew waited patiently as she tried to process the abrupt introduction of the subject of the two of them having children. He'd figured it was time to get to the heart of the kind of future they were likely to share.

Eventually, though, she shook her head as if to clear it. "Still not following," she admitted.

"We've never talked about kids before," he explained. "Do you want them? How many? I think it's an important thing for two people to discuss when they're getting serious about each other."

"Don't you think it's more important to discuss *if* they're getting serious about each other first?"

"I figured that goes without saying."

She shook her head. "There you go again, making assumptions. I agreed with you earlier that we're on track. We're not pulling into the station. I'm not there yet, Matthew." She gave him a chiding look. "Children? Really?"

"I'd like to have several," he said, pressing forward despite her obvious discomfort with the topic. He liked the blush he'd managed to bring to her cheeks. Keeping Laila off-kilter generally worked in his favor. She claimed to hate it, but he knew better. She thrived on the unpredictability of their relationship and the audaciousness of their conversations.

"I'm thinking five," he added. "I always envied the size of Uncle Mick's family."

"Envied?" she asked skeptically. "I thought you were just daunted because they outnumbered you, Susie and Luke."

"Which is why I want my kids to have a lot of backup. Since we don't know if Susie and Mack will wind up adopting—though my money's on that happening—and who knows what Luke might do, then expanding my side of the family could be up to us. What do you think?"

"I think you're certifiably crazy," she said.

"So, five's too many?"

"I mean you're crazy if you think I'm going to commit to anything like this now."

"It's a discussion, not a commitment. I'm just interested in how you feel about having kids in general."

She didn't look as if she believed him. "In general, I favor the idea of having kids," she said cautiously.

"How many? Two? Ten?"

"Three or four," she said eventually, picking numbers out of thin air just to end the subject.

He nodded. "I suppose I could compromise at four," he said agreeably. "See how good we are at this? Marriage is all about compromise, or so they tell me. Now let's talk about your dream house. What would it look like?"

"I haven't really given it a lot of thought," she claimed.

Matthew was skeptical. Didn't women start thinking about that kind of thing about five minutes after they started imagining the kind of wedding they wanted?

"Really? Heather certainly knew exactly what she wanted Driftwood Cottage to look like when Connor was having that remodeled for her. Uncle Mick said she had a whole folder crammed with pictures. And, believe me, Susie had very specific ideas for her house with Mack." He regarded her doubtfully. "You sure you've never thought about this?"

"I've thought about what I don't want," Laila admitted eventually. "I don't want a house that's so big and formal that people are scared to have fun in it."

"Like your parents' house," he guessed.

"Exactly," she said with a shiver. "I'm still surprised at the way Caitlyn and Carrie tear through the place without giving my mother a breakdown. I certainly never felt I could spill anything or leave my toys or schoolbooks lying around."

"How do you like Susie and Mack's place?"

Her eyes brightened. "What's not to love? The views of the water are completely awesome. You did an amazing job of making the rooms airy and bright, yet incredibly cozy." Her expression turned wistful. "I'd give anything to have a house on a piece of property by the bay."

Matthew smiled. "Good to know." Fortunately he had his own piece of property just like it a few feet down the shoreline, thanks to a very wise investment his father had made years ago. The land had been held for Susie, him and Luke. Now he knew exactly the kind of house to put on his lot, something similar to Susie's, but distinctive in its own ways.

He reached in his pocket for an ever-present piece of paper and pen, then began to sketch. "Something like this?" he asked, shoving the paper in Laila's direction.

Her eyes widened. "How did you do that with just a few strokes of a pen?"

"You like it?"

"Of course. It's amazing. I really love the porch and the huge sunroom."

"Anything you don't like?"

She shook her head. "You're a wonderful architect, Matthew. I'm sure it will be incredible. Where are you building it?"

"Next door to Susie and Mack." He held her gaze. "Eventually."

Once again, she looked startled. "You own the land next to theirs?"

"Technically Dad does, but he's giving each of us a piece of it. There will be a sizable lot for Luke whenever he's ready. Of course, if he persists in thinking he's crazy about Kristen Lewis, living two doors down from Susie and Mack could be awkward."

"When will you build your house?" Laila asked, her gaze still drawn to the sketch.

"When the time is right," he said evasively, then grinned. "That could be just around the corner."

"Matthew," she cautioned.

"Not getting ahead of myself," he insisted. "I'm just saying the property's there and, thanks to you, I have a rough idea of what to build on it."

"Sometimes you scare me," Laila said candidly.

"That's not my intention."

"I know that. It's just that you seem so certain about the future, about what you want, what you think is going to work out. How do you get to that place?" she asked wistfully.

"Do you really want to know?"

She nodded.

He touched a finger to her chin, forced her to meet his gaze, then said with quiet sincerity, "I look into your eyes. That's all, Laila. That's the secret. I look into your eyes and see everything I ever wanted."

Her throat worked at his words. A tear leaked out and spilled down her cheek.

"How am I supposed to resist you when you say things like that?" she whispered in a choked voice.

He smiled at her evident frustration. "You're not supposed to," he told her. "You're supposed to fall madly, passionately in love with me and live happily ever after."

"I want to," she admitted.

"What's holding you back?"

"The part of me that doesn't believe it's really possible for dreams to come true," she said.

"Give it time," he told her. "Mine certainly have."

He took her hand, felt her tremble. For a strong woman, she had so many vulnerabilities. He couldn't imagine why that was.

Oh, some of the blame could be laid at her father's feet, no doubt about that. Perhaps some belonged to the boys of Chesapeake Shores who'd been shorter than she was back in high school and hadn't wanted to risk the humiliation of being seen with her.

Some of the fault was probably even his. He had his own well-known track record with women. It was going to take more than sweet words and sincere declarations to convince her that his intentions were not only honorable, but lasting. That was okay, though, because he knew his own heart, even if she didn't.

"Let's dance," he said, pulling her to her feet.

It was a fast song, just what they needed to lighten the mood, but she held back.

"I'm not the world's best dancer," she warned. "I'm liable to step all over your feet. I'm renowned for my clumsiness."

Despite her voiced reluctance, her gaze as she looked

at the other couples on the floor was envious. Matthew persisted.

"I'm well-known for being quick on my feet," he countered. "And we're here where no one knows us. Who cares if we make complete spectacles of ourselves, as long as we're having fun?"

She smiled then and followed him to the dance floor, her movements perfectly in time to the music, if not terribly practiced.

"See," he said. "You're not half-bad."

"Which is barely more than half-good," she said, laughing. "Once again you've worked your magic. You've gotten me past my fear of looking ridiculous."

"That's my mission in life," he said solemnly. "I won't be happy till you see yourself as I do."

The music changed to something slow, and he drew her into his arms, held her close until she sighed and rested her head on his shoulder. It wasn't quite as good as getting her into his bed, but he understood why some people thought of dancing as the next best thing to making love in public. She fit him perfectly, moved with him exquisitely. And stirred him as no other woman had ever done. Stirred him a little too much, if the truth was told.

He gazed into her eyes. "Let's get out of here, okay?"

"And?"

"Go for a walk," he said nobly.

She smiled. "Is that what you really want to do?"

"No, but I know the rules. And to stick to them right now a long, chilly walk back to the hotel is just exactly what I need."

"I appreciate the effort," she said solemnly.

"I surely hope so, because this could kill me."

"I hope not, because I have big plans for you."

Startled, he looked into her laughing eyes. "Big plans?"

She nodded. "Eventually."

He sighed. "Now you're just tormenting me."

"Yes, I am," she said proudly.

He was glad she was happy about that, because he found it a little disturbing that she had that much power over him. Or maybe what really terrified him was knowing that he had absolutely no desire to run away. He was in this for the long haul, no question about it.

7

Nell had taken to slipping out of the hotel in the afternoon when everyone else assumed she was asleep in her room. She'd thought she was long past the days when sneaking around would appeal to her, but apparently even at her age she liked the idea of defying convention to slip off with a lover of whom her family disapproved.

Not that she and Dillon were lovers, of course. He'd stolen a few kisses, but that was more than enough for the time being. She couldn't imagine the idea of sex at her age. Then again, he was a robust, healthy man, so who knew what might happen down the road? If Mick was upset by her seeing Dillon, what on earth would he think if he knew where her thoughts were wandering these days? She chuckled as she tried to envision that conversation.

"What has you smiling?" Dillon asked, as he poured her tea in the back room of the tobacco shop.

"Just wondering what my son would think if he knew I wasn't sound asleep in my room at the hotel," she said.

To her surprise, Dillon frowned. "I'm not sure how happy I am about these secret meetings of ours. We've nothing to be ashamed of, Nell. I'd like to meet your family, get to know them."

"You've met Matthew," she reminded him, suddenly feeling defensive. "And Susie, of course."

"But not your sons," he said. "Clearly their opinions are the ones that really matter. I don't understand why you're so reluctant to introduce us."

Flustered by his apparent dismay, she set down her teacup and reached for his hand. "It's not that I'm ashamed or embarrassed or anything remotely like that," she assured him. "I think openness in a family is important. In fact, I was one of the first to speak out when I discovered that Matthew and Laila had been keeping their relationship a secret."

Momentarily distracted from their situation, Dillon regarded her with bewilderment. "They're so obviously in love. Why would they do such a thing?"

Nell shook her head. "I gather Laila was worried about the age difference and, to be honest, Matthew had a bit of a reputation as a ladies' man. She held a responsible position at her father's bank and worried that he would find fault."

She uttered a sigh. "As it turned out, that's exactly what happened. When Lawrence Riley discovered the truth, he ranted and raved about the appearance of impropriety, her lack of judgment and so on. Laila quit her job, then came to resent Matthew for the whole debacle.

They split up. This trip is an attempt at reconciliation, this time with everything out in the open."

Dillon gave her a thoughtful look. "And did you learn nothing from their experience?"

"Well, of course, I did," she said impatiently. "Didn't I just say that hiding things is a mistake?"

"And why does the same lesson not apply to us?"

She sighed. He had a point. She could hardly deny it. "It's just that Mick, my oldest son, has a view of me that doesn't allow for me being anything more than his mother and a grandmother to his children. I suppose it's always been true that children have difficulty seeing their parents as individual men and women with their own needs and desires and dreams. I'm pretty sure Mick thinks all of that ended for me when his father died."

"Do you suppose your other sons—Jeff and Thomas, is it—see it the same way?"

She smiled. "I doubt it. Thomas has just recently married for the third time. He'll be tolerant, if only because he expected the same from me. And Jeff is the most easygoing of all of them. He's also married to a very sensible woman." She paused, smiling. "So is Mick, for that matter, but Megan has a harder time getting through to him. His stubborn streak is legendary."

"I'd like to meet them all," Dillon said. "You won't be in Dublin forever, Nell. Before you know it, the holidays will be over and you'll be heading home."

Still she hesitated. In some ways she wanted to keep these stolen hours and days to herself, to create memories she could treasure, rather than deal with the risk of censure that was likely, at least from Mick. She wanted nothing to spoil this time.

"What is it now? What have you not said?" he asked.

"How would I explain you?" she asked simply.

A smile spread across his face then, and a booming laugh filled the small room.

"At our age, it's hard to imagine that we need to be explaining ourselves to anyone," he said, his lips twitching. "But you could start by telling them I'm an old friend. Or in the interest of total disclosure, an old flame." His grin spread. "Or perhaps as a potential lover."

She smiled. "That would definitely stir the pot, though I imagine Susie's filled them in on what she knows of our past history. It's the present I'm more concerned about, and suggesting that we might become lovers is most definitely a bad idea. I'm quite sure Mick would end up hospitalized right here in Dublin." She gave him a pointed look. "Perhaps with you right alongside him."

Dillon rested a hand against her cheek, his gaze softening. "Do we need a definition, Nell? We've a lot of feelings yet to explore, some old, some new. Until we've sorted them out, perhaps it's best to stick with friendship. That much is undeniable."

Ah, there it was, she thought, relaxing. Dillon was an old and dear friend who knew more of her past in Ireland than anyone else alive. There was a comfort in being with him, an ease that she'd never expected to find again. And the once-familiar twinkle in his eye, well, if that made her heart sing just a little, there was no reason to deny herself that.

She nodded slowly, coming to a decision. "Okay, my old *friend,* you'll join us tonight."

"I'll pick you up at the hotel, then," he said, looking pleased.

"You could meet us at the pub," she suggested.

"And leave room for anyone to think it was a chance encounter?" He shook his head. "There's an expression I've heard young people use, Nell. It's 'all-in.' *I'm* all-in, ready to go public. How about you?"

She hesitated one last time, then chuckled at the ridiculousness of it. She was in her eighties, not eighteen. She was the matriarch of this family, not a child to be watched over and controlled.

"Well, when you put it that way, what else is there to say?" she told him. "I'm all-in, too."

But she just might give Megan fair warning so she could prepare Mick and assure he'd be on his best behavior. Otherwise the Dublin skies were likely to be lit up with unexpected fireworks!

"I hear dinner tonight's a command performance," Laila said to Jess when she, Connie and Laila had once again gathered for tea and more girl talk. Today Susie had joined them as well, though thus far she'd been mostly silent. "Any idea what that's about?"

"Gram is bringing her beau," Susie announced, her eyes alight.

"Oh, you're all going to love him," Laila said. "He's a sweetheart."

Jess's gaze narrowed. "That's right, you and Susie have already met him. Is Dad right to be worried?"

"For a man who couldn't wait to marry off his children, Uncle Mick has some really old-fashioned ideas about Gram and romance," Susie replied. "Laila's been with them more recently than I have, but the look in Mr. O'Malley's eyes when he first saw Gram made me want to cry. It was so sweet. She said they were old friends, but I suspect there was a lot more to it that we don't know."

"Nell certainly seems very happy," Laila added. "They were so cute together the other day. When Matthew and I joined them at the café, they were actually holding hands. The minute they spotted us, they pulled away, as if we'd caught them misbehaving. Nell looked really guilty, but Mr. O'Malley just winked at us."

Jess continued to look worried. Connie frowned at her.

"Out with it, Jess. What's on your mind?" Connie asked. "Has Mick gotten to you?"

"No," Jess insisted. "I guess I can't help thinking, though, about what would happen if Gram really does fall in love—or back in love—with this old flame and decides to move to Ireland."

The suggestion, which hadn't even occurred to Laila, silenced all of them.

"I never even thought of that," Susie admitted. "What would we do without Gram? She's so much a part of all of our lives."

"Lots of people have no relationship at all with their grandparents," Connie reminded her. "Jake never knew ours. Only our mom's mother was still alive when I was born, but she died before I turned two, so I barely remember her."

"But this is *Gram*," Jess said. "She practically raised me, Abby, Bree, Kevin and Connor. And what about Sunday dinners and holidays? You know she's the only reason my dad, Uncle Jeff and Uncle Thomas have managed to stay civil all these years."

"They're all on better terms now," Laila said, trying to soothe her. She could see that Jess was genuinely terrified of things changing so dramatically. Even Susie looked shaken.

"And it's way too soon to be thinking about any of this," Connie added. "Nell's bringing him to dinner, not announcing an engagement."

Jess's eyes widened with alarm. "Oh, no, what if that's it? What if she insisted on everyone being there tonight so she could announce her engagement? Remember what she said right before the trip, Susie, that she was going to make sure someone walked down the aisle."

Susie gave her a pointed look. "I think she was referring to someone else," she said, nodding in Laila's direction.

Though Susie probably thought she was being subtle, Laila caught on. She regarded Susie with shock. "Me? She wanted Matthew and me to walk down the aisle?"

"She was *hoping,*" Susie corrected. "We all were."

Laila immediately went from trying to sympathize with their concern over Nell to protecting herself from their scheming. "That's why you've been pushing so hard for Matthew and me to reconcile. You want a wedding?" she asked, her voice climbing. "Here? While we're in Dublin?"

Susie shrugged. "It seems romantic."

"Oh, sweet heaven," she murmured. "Does Matthew know what you all are up to?"

"It was his idea," Susie blurted, then winced. "Before."

"Before what?"

"Before you broke up with him," Susie explained. "That sort of put a damper on the plan."

"He had a plan?" Laila asked, her mind reeling. "An actual, formal plan?"

"He *did,*" Susie corrected. "I'm not sure about now. Maybe. I don't know. I've been trying to get a fix on things, but you've both shut me down." She gave Laila an accusatory look, as if her lack of insight were all Laila's fault.

Jess shook her head. "Way to muddy the waters, Suze. Get your foot out of your mouth and let's focus on Gram."

Connie ignored her and focused on Laila. "You okay? You look a little pale."

Laila forced a smile. "I'm just swell," she lied. People were planning her entire future behind her back, but no big deal, right? They were planning a *wedding!* She'd always known the O'Briens had a certain amount of audacity, but this was too much. She'd never heard of a surprise wedding, but if any family had the outrageousness and confidence to try to pull one off, this one did.

Wishing it were something much, much stronger, she picked up her tea and finished it in one long swallow. When that didn't help, she picked up the Devon cream and a spoon and finished that off, too.

"Um, usually that goes on a scone," Connie suggested gently.

"And usually people ask the prospective bride before they plan a wedding," she retorted.

"It's not planned," Susie told her hurriedly. "It was just an idea, a wish, something we all knew Matthew wanted."

"And, of course, O'Briens always get what they want," Laila said, not sure whether to laugh or scream. She stood up. "I need to go."

"To your room?" Connie asked hopefully.

"No, home, or maybe anyplace in the entire world where there are no O'Briens."

Susie stood up and blocked her path, looking genuinely scared. "You can't. Please, Laila. Matthew will kill me if you leave now. Don't punish him because I've got a big mouth."

Laila understood her concern. Matthew would be furious if Laila took off and he discovered why. That, however, was not her concern.

All she cared about right now was getting as far away from Dublin as humanly possible before Matthew so much as hinted at a quickie wedding right here in Ireland. She was very much afraid that if the subject came up, she'd be powerless to resist the whole wonderfully impulsive, romantic, crazy idea of it.

And as much as she relished the impulsive side of her nature that Matthew drew out, she knew with every fiber of her being that marriage was definitely not something to be rushed into or taken lightly.

Matthew was a little taken aback when Mack and Luke tracked him down just as he was returning from doing some last-minute Christmas shopping. With the holiday only two days away and a family the size of his, shopping was a time-consuming task. They actually cornered him on the street and steered him directly into the hotel bar.

"What has gotten into the two of you?" he demanded.

"Why haven't you been answering your cell phone?" Luke countered. "We've been trying to call you for the past hour."

"The battery's probably dead," Matthew admitted. "I forgot to charge it last night. What's so urgent?"

"It's Laila," Mack said.

Matthew stilled. "What about her? She didn't step off the curb into oncoming traffic or something, did she?" It was all too easy to do with cars whizzing past on what for them was the wrong side of the street. He'd done it himself to near-disastrous results a time or two.

"She's fine," Luke said. "Alive, anyway."

He frowned. "What are you talking about?"

"She may be packing up to go back to Chesapeake Shores," Mack said.

Now Matthew was glad he was sitting down. He only wished the drink he wanted was handy, but the waiter hadn't even checked on them yet. "Home?" he repeated. "What the hell happened around here today? Why would she want to go home? Everything was fine the last time I saw her. Better than fine, in fact."

"Don't freak out, now, okay?" Mack said soothingly. "It's not as if Susie were trying to get into your business or anything."

His blood started to simmer. Whatever was going on, it couldn't possibly be good if his sister was involved and Mack was trying to come up with excuses for her even before he offered an explanation.

"One of you needs to start talking," he said tightly.

"Or I swear I will strangle both of you without a second's hesitation."

"Which means you'd never get answers," Luke pointed out, then winced at Matthew's fierce scowl. "I'm just saying…"

"The girls," Mack began.

"Susie, Connie, Jess and Laila," Luke added, suddenly eager to fill in the blanks.

"They went out for tea this afternoon," Mack concluded.

Matthew drew in a deep breath. That didn't sound so awful, but from the expressions on his brother and brother-in-law's faces, whatever had happened wasn't some innocent little gabfest.

"And?" he prodded.

"It sort of came out that everyone was hoping you and Laila would get married in Ireland," Luke said in a rush.

Matthew looked from one man to the other. "How the hell does something like that sort of casually come up in the conversation?"

Mack sighed. "I'm not real clear on the details. Susie was too upset, but I gather once it was out there, Laila freaked."

"Big-time," Luke confirmed.

"She says she's going home," Mack added. "Or maybe to some O'Brien-free zone."

Matthew was immediately on his feet, all thoughts of a drink and everything else forgotten. "Has she left the hotel?"

"I don't think so," Luke said. "I've been hanging out in the lobby keeping an eye out for her and for you."

"And I stopped at the front desk," Mack said. "She didn't check out of the room."

Matthew nodded. At least there was some good news. Still, he cast a hard look at Mack. "Tell my sister I will deal with her later."

Mack shook his head. "No, you won't. She's beside herself as it is. Stress isn't good for her."

Matthew thought of the cancer she'd beat only recently. He thought Susie was far tougher than Mack was giving her credit for, but he had no desire to test that belief. Nor did he especially want to physically tangle with his brother-in-law, an ex-jock who remained in excellent shape. Not that he wasn't in good condition himself, but a brawl would only give him momentary satisfaction. It wouldn't win Laila's heart.

"I'm going to Laila's room," he told them, shoving his packages at Luke. "Take these upstairs for me, okay?"

"Done," Luke said at once.

"And I'll hang out down here a little longer just in case Laila comes down while you're heading up," Mack offered.

Matthew nodded. "Thanks."

Even as he crossed the lobby, he wondered what on earth he was going to say to calm Laila down. He could hardly deny that the idea of a wedding here in Ireland had crossed his mind. He'd brought the engagement ring with him. His grandmother had assured him she knew all about getting a special license. Heck, he'd even enlisted his own mother to check out a few bridal stores. The plan had definitely been in place. It was a true testament to hope over reality.

The one thing he hadn't counted on was someone else springing the idea on her. Laila was making strides in becoming impetuous and daring, but this was some sort of giant leap in the unpredictability department. She was still taking baby steps.

Just as the elevator doors opened on her floor, he saw the door to her room open a crack. She poked her head out for a quick look in each direction, then sighed heavily when she spotted him.

"You wouldn't be trying to sneak off, would you?" he inquired lightly, walking right past her into her room and closing the door behind him. He eyed the suitcases by the door. "I guess that answers my question."

"Coming to Ireland was a mistake," she said.

"Have you been having a bad time?"

"Of course not, but—"

"Are you mad at me again?"

She hesitated over that one.

He smiled. "Let me rephrase. Are you furious with me for something I've actually done?"

She peered at him doubtfully. "You're making some kind of distinction there. Explain what you're getting at."

"I've made a few mistakes with you since we met. I'm sure you could probably list them all. But most of those happened before this trip, and I was under the impression we came here with a clean slate. Clear enough so far?"

She nodded, though she didn't look especially happy about it.

He nodded as well. "So, have I done something specific since we arrived that upset you? If so, I'd like to set it right."

"You've been planning our wedding behind my back," she accused in a huff. "Who does that? Aside from an O'Brien, I mean. No one else on earth would have that kind of audacity."

"I haven't exactly planned our wedding," he replied. "Haven't even proposed, as a matter of fact."

"No, you haven't, which is precisely my point. People do not go around planning weddings for people who aren't even engaged. It's ridiculous."

"A few people in the family might have gotten a little ahead of themselves," he admitted. "They love you. They like me enough to want me to be happy. They got carried away. It's hardly a crime. It's not as if they could make either of us do anything we haven't agreed to, now, could they?"

She sat down on the edge of the bed, a scowl firmly in place. "I just don't like it, that's all."

"Understandable. Hearing about it must have been a shock."

"It was infuriating, if you must know."

"I can imagine."

She eyed him suspiciously. "Are you trying to placate me?"

"Pretty much. I'd hate to have you let some offhand comment from my sister ruin the rest of this trip for you."

"How'd you find out about this anyway? Did Susie confess?"

"Actually Mack and Luke found out. They've been

staking out the lobby waiting for me to get back and hoping to keep you from leaving before we talked."

"Ah, the infamous Brotherhood of the O'Briens." It didn't sound complimentary the way she said it.

Still, Matthew laughed. "We do stick together. It can be a good thing, Laila."

"It can also be annoying and intimidating. I felt as if I were just minutes from being stuffed into some lacy white dress and marched down the aisle."

He gave her a thorough once-over that brought color to her cheeks. "Nah, you're not the lacy type. I see you in white satin, something all sleek and sensuous."

She opened her mouth, then snapped it shut and stared at him. "You've been thinking about how I'll look on our wedding day?"

"Of course I have. It's quite a vision." He held her gaze. "You're beautiful. You take my breath away under normal conditions. In a wedding gown, there's a good chance you could stop my heart."

She blinked, then sighed. "You have to stop saying things like that, Matthew. I can't think straight when you do."

"Thinking straight can be highly overrated," he said.

"Not about this," she retorted firmly. "Marriage is serious. It's forever. People need to think it through. If more people did, there would be fewer divorces. Ask Connor."

"Connor's currently on the happily-married band-wagon," Matthew reminded her. "His particular brand of cynicism is a thing of the past. Want me to call him so he can give you a testimonial?"

She frowned. "You're not taking me seriously."

"Actually I am. Believe me, I get why this whole business upset you. You like feeling in control. It's who you are. And you may enjoy the occasional wild and reckless ride we're on, but you're not quite ready to trust the woman you are with me."

She seemed surprised by his assessment. "Something like that."

"It's okay. I promised you no pressure on this trip."

"Having people think we might end the trip with a wedding ceremony is a *lot* of pressure."

"I know. I'm sorry."

"Then you'll tell them to back off, to rein in all the craziness?"

"I'll tell them," he promised.

He just didn't expect it to do any good, because the one thing other than stubbornness that was in the O'Brien genes was meddling. He was surrounded by a bunch of die-hard romantics. Today that had proved to be a serious disadvantage. By the end of the trip... well, he was still counting on it working out in his favor.

The one thing he understood about Laila that she didn't yet understand about herself was that she wanted desperately to have exactly that kind of unpredictable, heart-stopping romance in her life. And her best chance for it was most definitely with him.

Mick put on a tie, then yanked it off. "Why am I getting dressed up as if this is some special occasion?" he asked Megan irritably. "What is Ma up to, anyway, insisting that everyone be there tonight?"

Megan gave him a soothing look. "You know perfectly well why she wants us all to be together tonight. She's bringing a date."

Mick saw red at the reminder. As if his mother had any business dating at her age. And, of all people, some man she hadn't seen in sixty years or more, if the story was to be believed that she'd left him behind to marry Mick's father. What was she thinking? It was only going to end badly.

"If she thinks I'm going to show up and give them my blessing, then she really has lost her mind," he growled.

Megan crossed the room and stood directly in front of him, hands on hips. Despite the difference in their sizes, she was capable of being intimidating when she wanted to be.

"You will be on your very best behavior tonight, Mick O'Brien. I mean it. You will not embarrass Nell."

"I won't have to. She's embarrassing herself."

Megan's eyes flashed. "Nonsense! And if you can't change your attitude, then perhaps you ought to stay right here and sulk like the petulant two-year-old who seems to have taken over your body."

Stunned by the accusation, Mick stared at her. "Petulant two-year-old?" he echoed.

"No better than your namesake, though even little Mick is getting past the tantrum stage."

He sat down on the edge of the bed, considering her words, then sighed. "You're right, as usual," he conceded. "I'm just worried about her, Meggie. It's not like Ma to act all fluttery around some man none of us even know. She's not some young girl."

Megan chuckled. "No, she certainly isn't. She's a grown woman who knows her own mind. She raised three amazing sons, then served as a surrogate mother to our children after I'd left. No one could do that without being sensible and wise." She met his gaze. "Agreed?"

He wrestled with his conscience, then nodded. "Agreed."

"And it's not as if this man is someone she met just a few days ago. I gather she was once quite serious about him."

"Years ago," Mick reminded her. "They were little more than teenagers then. Who knows the kind of man he's become?"

"Which is precisely why you and the others will use this evening to get to know him. Your opinions and advice will mean a lot more to Nell if they're coming from someone who's actually knowledgeable when it comes to Dillon O'Malley, and not leaping to conclusions based on fear."

His gaze narrowed. "Fear? When have I ever been afraid of anything?"

"Only once before that I've ever seen, when Nell had pneumonia years ago and we all thought we might lose her. You have that same terrified look about you now. Don't you know that she'll continue to be a part of our lives no matter what happens with Dillon O'Malley?" She regarded him pointedly. "At least she will if you don't force her to choose."

He pulled his wife onto his lap. "How'd you get to be so smart?" he asked, his tension easing as he held her.

She grinned. "I've always been smart. You just pay a little more attention to me now."

"Could be," he agreed. "I won't make the mistake of ignoring you again." He ran his fingers through the short cap of frosted curls that made her look like a girl. "You ground me, Meggie. I hope you know how much I love you, have always loved you."

Her hand rested against his cheek, her touch gentle. "I never questioned your feelings, Mick. Not once. It was only your priorities that tore us apart for a while."

"But we're good now?"

"Better than good," she said with a smile, then tweaked his nose. "Unless you do something to make me change my mind tonight."

He laughed and set her on her feet. "Best behavior, I promise." No matter what it cost him.

After the day she'd had, Laila wasn't especially eager to spend the evening in a roomful of O'Briens, but her curiosity about how the family would react to Nell and Dillon's romance won out. If nothing else, she could provide the couple with some backup if the environment was hostile. She probably had a clearer view of what it was like to be caught in the family headlights than anyone else, especially after today's revelations.

Reluctantly, she agreed to walk to the pub with Matthew.

"Just so you understand that no one is to get the impression that we're reconciled or that the plan is moving forward," she warned.

"Message received," he said, though there seemed to be a twinkle in his eye when he said it.

The light drizzle that had made the day damp and dreary had ended earlier, so the walk was pleasant. Inside the pub, there was a decided atmosphere of merriment. A fire was blazing in the hearth, and a band was already warming up with a promised repertoire of Irish tunes.

Mick had booked a private room that still allowed access to the pub's main room. It, too, had a fire going, but in there the atmosphere was decidedly strained. Laila glanced around. There was no sign yet of Nell and her date.

"Where's your grandmother?" she asked Matthew after surveying the roomful of O'Briens and their spouses and children.

"Probably waiting to make a grand entrance," he said. "Or perhaps she came to her senses and decided to have dinner with Dillon somewhere else."

"Nell's no coward," Laila chided.

"No, she's not," he agreed, then nodded toward the doorway. "There's the happy couple now."

Laila deliberately caught Nell's eye and gave her an encouraging smile, then winked at Dillon. Both of them seemed to relax.

"Going over to the enemy?" Matthew whispered in her ear.

"I like Dillon," she replied. "I thought you did, too."

"I do. I'm just not sure how wise it is to make that clear with this crowd. I sense some hostility."

Laila gave him a disgusted look and crossed the room. "Why don't I take your coats?" she said cheerfully, since no one else had stepped forward.

Nell gave her a grateful smile. "Thank you, Laila."

Susie rushed over to join them. "Hi, Gram. Mr. O'Malley."

"It's Dillon, please," he said, giving her a warm smile.

"Let me take you over and introduce you to my parents," Susie said. "Gram, maybe Laila can get you something to drink."

"Of course," Laila said at once. "What would you like?"

Nell's gaze followed Susie and Dillon. "Perhaps I should go with him. I know the family's divide-and-conquer tactics all too well."

Laila smiled. "Dillon will win them over. I've no doubt of that. And Jeff and Jo aren't the problem. Susie will see that they're on his side, so there will be plenty of backup before Mick has his say."

Nell nodded. "I suppose you're right," she said, though there was still a note of concern in her voice. "I'll just keep a close eye on things. In the meantime, I believe I'd like a Bulmers cider if they have it. I have a feeling anything more alcoholic than that would be unwise tonight."

"I'm on it," Laila said, relieved to see that Megan was heading Nell's way with a reassuring look on her face.

"And so it begins," Matthew intoned, joining her at the bar. "Maybe there won't be bloodshed after all. Mick may be scowling, but he doesn't look as if he has any murderous intent."

Laila rolled her eyes at his feeble attempt at a joke, then handed him the Bulmers. "Take this to your grandmother. Show her your support. I'm going over to Dillon just in case things get tense between him and Mick."

"Jeff, Jo and Thomas are there now," Matthew said. "They'll keep Mick in check."

"All the same, I'll feel better if I'm nearby to help Dillon make a quick getaway."

Matthew frowned. "Is this the way it's to be tonight, with you darting off on various missions that will keep us apart?"

"Entirely likely," she told him unrepentantly, then followed suit by walking away.

She told herself it was better to keep a safe distance between them. Despite her knee-jerk response to the whole impromptu wedding notion, she was entirely too susceptible to Matthew lately. Far from Chesapeake Shores, her father and the bank that was such a bone of contention between them, it had become increasingly difficult to recall why being with Matthew was such a terrible idea. *His* family at least clearly embraced the idea of a union between them.

Still, when it came time for dinner, she managed to slip into a seat between Connie and Thomas on one side and Jess and Will on the other. Matthew gave her an amused look from across the room, then settled at a table with his parents, along with Susie, Mack and Luke.

Though the door between this room and the main room of the pub had been shut to lessen the noise during dinner, someone reopened it as soon as the meal was over. The sound of the band drifted in, and soon the O'Briens were singing along with gusto. Laila caught Nell with a nostalgic expression on her face. She smiled when Dillon leaned in to whisper something in her ear.

"I think we need to try our luck on the dance floor," Thomas said to Connie. "I believe I can remember a few of the steps I was taught."

Connie regarded him skeptically. "Are you sure? I've never learned to do an Irish jig."

"Then I won't be making too big a fool of myself in front of you, will I?" Thomas said, drawing her away from the table.

As soon as they'd left, Jess and Will wandered off, as well. Laila felt someone slip into the vacant seat next to hers and knew instinctively it was Matthew. He'd just been waiting for this opportunity to present itself.

"We're taking bets on how long it will be before Uncle Mick's head explodes," he said, nodding in his uncle's direction.

Laila laughed. "He is looking fiercely protective,

isn't he? Still, he hasn't caused a scene tonight. He should get some recognition for that."

"Dad believes Mick's more worried about how our lives will change if Gram stays in Dublin than he is about the possibility that her heart might be broken."

"I've heard something similar from Susie and from Jess. They're scared Nell will decide to stay." She met his gaze. "How about you?"

"I wouldn't much like it, but I'm more worried that the whole thing is doomed. He has a business here. She's coming home with us next week."

"Love always finds a way, Matthew, at least when it's right."

He looked surprised by her comment. "You believe that? I thought you'd grown cynical."

"Of course I do. I think most women believe that or want to, unless they've been deeply hurt by someone."

"And yet you walked away from what we had just because it got a little complicated."

She sighed at the characterization. Besides, weren't they past this now? "It was more than a little complicated," she said patiently. "I gave up my career because my father disapproved of us."

"You quit in a huff, then resented me because of it," he reminded her. "Somehow you've managed to forget that I tried to stop you, but you weren't willing to spend some time trying to turn his opinion around."

"Because it was hopeless," she said stubbornly. "Besides, my father's low opinion of me went back further than that. I was only in that job because Trace manipulated my father into giving it to me." She met his gaze. "Do you have any idea how much that hurt, Matthew?"

"Of course I do. I know what it's like to disappoint someone you love."

She wasn't sure of that. "Really? Who?"

"You," he said. "Maybe if I'd fought harder for us, you wouldn't have found it so easy to walk away. And if I'd been a better man, had less of a roving eye, maybe your father would have approved of me."

She was startled that he was blaming himself for any of what had happened. As he'd just noted, her blaming him was unjustified. "Maybe both of us need to stop casting any kind of blame. You didn't create the situation, Matthew. It was me. I showed poor judgment in having some casual fling with you. I let myself be carried away by the moment. If I'd been thinking at all—"

He cut her off. "Way to deliver a blow, Laila. Are you suggesting that no woman in her right mind would get involved with a guy like me?"

"No, of course not," she said, rattled. "You're a great guy, just the wrong one for someone in the position I held at the bank."

He gave her an amused look. "Because I'm an O'Brien?"

She found the deliberately teasing question annoying. "Don't be ridiculous. The town adores and respects all things O'Brien."

"Then it's because I'm an architect following in Uncle Mick's footsteps."

She frowned. "Of course not!"

"Then what? Is it because I dated a lot of women? That's what men do when they're single. Last I heard, it wasn't a crime."

"Oh, for heaven's sake, you know perfectly well I

wasn't suggesting that. It's only your dating record combined with your age that made you inappropriate for me. The way my dad saw it, we were risking a scandal."

"You seemed to be enjoying our scandalous behavior every bit as much as I did," he reminded her.

She sighed. "I can't deny that."

He gave her a satisfied nod. "Now we're getting somewhere. Most people would have fought for what we had, proved it meant more than what anyone assumed. It seems to me the only thing you did was prove your father right."

She regarded him with shock. "Excuse me?"

"The going got tough, and what did you do? You ran. You walked away from the job and from me. Quite the double whammy, wouldn't you say?"

"It sounds as if your opinion of me isn't any better than my father's," she said. "Tell me again why you think we should waste time trying to reconcile?"

Even as she spoke, she was gathering her purse and gloves, preparing to leave.

"There you go again, running just because I said something you didn't like."

Because of the taunt, she made herself stand her ground, fury causing her to tremble. He was on his feet, as well.

"Matthew O'Brien, are you calling me a coward?"

"If the shoe fits…" He held her gaze, then said quietly, "Dance with me."

"What?" she asked, incredulous at the out-of-the-blue, poorly timed request.

"We seem to communicate much better when you're in my arms," he explained.

"That's no way to resolve our problems," she insisted, but with his hand outstretched and his gaze steady, she found it impossible to resist. "Fine. Whatever."

But even before they'd taken a step toward the dance floor, she knew she'd made a mistake. Picking a fight with him had felt a whole lot safer. She'd never been able to think straight in his arms.

He hesitated, obviously disconcerted that she'd accepted his invitation, albeit ungraciously. "Really?"

She gave him an impatient look. "It's a dance, Matthew, not an invitation to bed."

A wicked gleam lit his eyes. "We'll see about that."

Despite the deliberate challenge in that comment, Laila felt herself relax once she was in his arms. It felt so good to be close to him again…so dangerously tempting. The sparks were flying all over the place, but she felt safe, too. Cherished, even. It was surprising, given how annoyed she'd been with him just moments ago.

"You still sure about not joining me in bed?" he inquired, the teasing question a whisper against her cheek.

She allowed herself a smile. He was such a guy! "You were the one who declared this trip a sex-free vacation. And not ten minutes ago you were berating me for having no gumption. What would your opinion of me be if I allowed you into my bed after all those promises we made before we left home?"

"I'd still respect you in the morning," he said. His expression was somber, but his eyes were twinkling.

She laughed, then sobered. "Seriously, Matthew, after what you said a little while ago, why would you still want to sleep with me? It sounded as if you think I'm spineless."

"Sorry," he said with apparent regret. "I was trying to make a point about how easily you backed away from conflict, when I know you're stronger than that. You're also a complicated, exciting, desirable woman. I can't even look at you without wanting you so badly it makes my whole body ache with it," he said frankly, allowing his hand to slide from its respectable spot on her back to someplace suggestively lower.

There it was, the open declaration that made her feel like all of those things, a view she'd never held of herself before they'd gotten together. They were heady words for a woman who'd accepted that she was every bit as stodgy as the parents to whom she was so frequently compared.

It would be so easy to say yes to Matthew tonight. That was the problem, though. She'd said yes too quickly from the beginning, established a pattern that was filled with heat and no demands or expectations. For a long time it had satisfied both of them.

Now it was clear that Matthew wanted more. She knew it. So did his entire meddling family. He'd transformed from lusty playboy to a man ready to settle down and play by all the rules. Laila was still trying to catch up.

"No," she said, the word little more than a reluctant whisper. She looked into his eyes with regret. "I can't do this, Matthew. I'm sorry. I don't want to go back to the way things were."

"Neither do I," he insisted. "I want us to take the next step forward."

The trouble with that was, she thought, it was even more terrifying. She left his arms hurriedly, grabbed

her gloves, purse and coat and exited the pub, walking
as fast as she could to escape him, to escape her confused thoughts, and most of all to escape the desire that
once more was simply too much for her.

"Go after her, you idiot," Luke said when Matthew
walked to the bar and ordered another pint of ale.

"That's the last thing she wants tonight," Matthew
told his brother. He knew perfectly well that Laila had
deliberately picked a fight with him to slow things down
because she was scared not only of her feelings, but all
the pressure from everyone else who was determined
to see them married.

"All women want to be pursued," Luke said with
surprising conviction for a man barely out of college.

Despite his age, though, Luke had made a practice
of emulating Matthew and their brother-in-law Mack,
both of whom had well-known reputations for casual
flirtations. Luke, however, seemed to have added an
element of wisdom that had eluded Matthew, at least.

Still it was difficult for Matthew to take his little
brother's opinions all that seriously. "Says the man
who's in Dublin alone."

"Only out of respect for our sister," Luke said. "I
spoke to Kristen just tonight, and she'll be flying over
to meet me as soon as the rest of you take off for home.
We'll start the New Year together."

Matthew frowned. The news was not only unexpected, it was distressing. He didn't trust the woman.
He knew she'd deliberately tried to work her way back
into Mack's affections, even knowing that he was married and Susie had cancer.

"It's that serious?" he asked Luke worriedly.

Luke shrugged. "Not a word I'd choose," he insisted. "I can't be a hundred percent sure yet, but it has potential. Maybe watching all the rest of you fall in love has influenced me, but I like the way Kristen challenges me. She's not even close to what I expected."

"And have you taken our sister's feelings into consideration?"

"Of course," Luke said. "Didn't I just say that Kristen's not here because of Susie?"

"Suze won't be one bit happier if she finds out later that the two of you are together."

"Hey, I'll worry about that if things do start getting serious. Right now we're just together off and on, sort of like you and Laila."

Matthew bristled. "It's not like that for Laila and me," he said heatedly.

Luke didn't back down. "We both know it was," he said.

"Well, things change."

"She walked out of here alone, didn't she? And you let her go. If you ask me, somebody's still playing games."

"Well, it's not me," Matthew insisted.

"Laila, then?"

"No. Geez, you're a pain," he said in exasperation.

Luke grinned. "Only because you know I speak the truth. If you want her, you're going to have to fight to prove it. Sitting here with me and licking your wounds isn't going to cut it."

Reluctantly, Matthew had to admit he had a point.

"Thanks for the advice and for the pint," he told his brother, then walked off whistling.

"Hey, who said I was buying?" Luke called after him. "You owe me for straightening you out."

"Only if this works out," Matthew said.

His upbeat attitude was all for show, though. Realistically he thought there was a very good chance that Laila would slam her hotel room door in his face.

9

The brisk walk back to the hotel had calmed Laila's temper and left her filled with regret. Oh, she knew she'd been wise to walk away from Matthew without leaving even the tiniest opening for him to seduce her tonight, but it hadn't been easy. Her body was practically humming with desire.

Rather than going directly to the hotel, she kept walking. The streets were still busy, and she felt safe enough walking along Grafton Street to do a little window shopping. Lights twinkled merrily in shop windows along with holiday displays that reminded her of those back home. Many of these had a more old-fashioned look to them, with caroling figures dressed in fur-trimmed velvet, piles of artificial snow and scenes of children anxiously awaiting the arrival of St. Nicholas.

She circled around and paused to smile at the statue of Molly Malone, which seemed to be a huge tourist draw judging from the people having their pictures taken with it.

She was barely halfway down the final block leading back to the hotel when she saw Matthew. His expression was slightly frantic as he talked with one of the hotel doormen. Wondering what on earth might have happened to upset him so, she instinctively hurried forward.

"Matthew, is everything okay? Did something happen after I left the party?"

When he whirled at the sound of her voice, then saw her, his entire body seemed to relax. "There you are," he said, his relief unmistakable.

The doorman gave her a wink. "I think he was fearing you'd run out on him."

She studied Matthew. "Is he right? Did you think I'd left for home?"

"When you didn't answer the door to your room, yes," he admitted. "It's not as if you hadn't threatened to do just that earlier today."

"I went for a walk. Nothing more."

"Well, you took ten years off my life," he told her. He gave her a speculative look. "The least you can do now is have a nightcap with me."

She allowed herself a smile. "Really? The least I can do?"

He nodded. "It'll be a start."

"I probably shouldn't ask what you have in mind for payback after that."

He grinned. "Probably not." He gave the doorman a tip. "Thanks for trying to reassure me that she was still in the neighborhood."

"I told you she'd greeted me as she passed by, now,

didn't I?" the man said. "And that she had no luggage. I keep an eye out for our guests. It's part of the job." He gave Laila a broad smile before assuring Matthew, "And I've been at this a long time. You're not the first to fear they've been abandoned. Now that you've been reunited, the two of you should enjoy the rest of your evening."

"We will," Laila responded.

"Nice man," Matthew said as he steered Laila inside and toward the bar. He gave her a hopeful look. "Unless you'd rather have that nightcap upstairs?"

"The bar suits me fine," she said.

After they were seated and had ordered Irish coffees to take away the night's chill, Matthew met her gaze.

"I'm sorry about earlier," he said earnestly. "I just get so frustrated sometimes that you apparently can't see what I see when I look at the two of us. It seems we're always taking a few steps forward, then an equal number back."

Curious, she asked, "What do you see, and try to keep it PG-rated, if you don't mind."

He laughed at that. "Now, see, there's precisely the problem. You seem to recall only what the two of us are like in bed, while I've always viewed the whole package."

"Matthew, there was no whole package," she protested. "We didn't do anything except sneak off to your place for sex."

He held her gaze. "And whose fault was that?" he challenged.

"Mine," she admitted readily. "But if we go back down that road, we'll only argue some more." She studied him closely. "Were you honestly able to view that period when we were together some other way?"

"I wouldn't be half so upset about our breakup if we'd only been about the sex, Laila. You know my history. If that was all it was about, I had options."

She grimaced at the reminder. "Okay, what was different with me? How did you know it wasn't just your usual pattern of falling into and out of bed with one more woman?"

His gaze was direct and unflinching. "Because I wanted you to stay," he said simply. "I never tired of being with you. I looked forward to catching at least a glimpse of you at family functions. I never got this panicky feeling that things were moving too fast with us. If anything, I thought things were progressing too slowly."

She smiled at that. On the first night they'd bumped into each other at Brady's, things had gone from simmer to boiling in a matter of minutes, it seemed. After years of their being nothing more than casual friends, sparks had flown.

"I wanted more," he continued. "I always wanted more. From our first night together, I knew I'd never have enough of you. And not just in bed," he added hurriedly. "I like the way your mind works. I like that you have goals and ambitions, and it killed me that I was even partially responsible for your walking away from one of those goals."

The sincerity behind his words was unmistakable. Laila allowed every word to seep into her heart, warming a spot that had grown cold and fearful. She wanted to believe him, *needed* to believe him. And yet trusting that something that had begun so impulsively and had ended so badly could possibly be right was terrifying.

"What are you thinking?" he asked.

She held her fingers a scant quarter inch apart. "That I'm this close to believing you."

"How close are you to risking everything and jumping back into this relationship?"

She widened the gap between her fingers ever so slightly.

He nodded, grinning. "That's pretty good given the chasm between us not that long ago."

She smiled. "Not just pretty good. It's a miracle."

"'Tis the season," he said lightly.

Laila laughed. "So they say."

"Care to go upstairs and see if we can close that gap?" he inquired, his eyes filled with daring.

"Now, that," she said firmly, "would take more than a miracle."

It would take a leap of faith she had no idea if she could manage.

"Can I at least walk you to your room and sneak a good-night kiss?" he asked hopefully.

"I wouldn't say no to that," she told him, already a little breathless just at the thought of it. "But *outside* the door," she added very firmly.

"Laila Riley, you don't think I'd try to take advantage of you, do you?" he asked with mock dismay.

"In a heartbeat," she responded.

What worried her more was that she might let him.

"I thought the evening went very well," Dillon said as he walked Nell back to the hotel.

She regarded him with amusement. "You're quite the optimist, aren't you?"

"There was no bloodshed," he protested. "I consider that an excellent sign. Even Mick, though he looked as if he wanted to wring my neck a time or two, held his tongue and behaved with considerable reserve and good manners."

"That was, indeed, a blessing," Nell agreed. "I think we can thank Megan for that. My daughter-in-law has a talent for getting her way with him and coaxing him into a more reasonable frame of mind."

"Because he obviously adores her. You say they were separated for a time?"

"Divorced," she corrected. "And it was for years. They've only been reconciled and remarried for a year now. The wedding was last New Year's Eve. There was some doubt it would happen even then, because Connor disapproved and Megan wanted all of the children not only at the ceremony, but happy for them."

"Well, obviously they've all come to peaceful terms now," Dillon said. He gave her a warm look. "It's a wonderful family, Nell, and I can see how much they all adore and respect you. You're a vital part of their lives."

"And grateful for it," she said with feeling, then regarded him intently. "We haven't talked nearly as much about your family, Dillon. Aren't you close?"

He sighed at the question. "Our only child, our daughter, was a rebellious young woman. She and her mother fought over everything. If my wife said the sky was blue, then Kiera said it was gray. The battles started at an early age and never lessened. As Kiera got older, the fights became about more important things such as the way she was living her life. I didn't approve of her choices, either, but I could see we were only driving her away. Eventually she moved out of the house, then out of town. She cut off all ties."

Nell's eyes filled with tears at the thought of losing a child in such a way. "Dillon, I'm so sorry."

"It was a terrible time," he said with feeling. "But I sought her out when her mother got sick, warned her not to let things end with such a rift between them, told her she'd never forgive herself. She was a mother herself by then, so she understood what I was saying. She came back, mended fences. It was a beautiful thing to see the two of them, heads together, laughing before the end came."

"And now?" Nell asked.

"We see each other often. Her children, like your grandchildren, are the lights of my life. And in a bit of irony, her daughter is every bit as headstrong as our Kiera. No one tells our Moira what to do."

Nell could imagine it. Those were the sort of chickens that often came home to roost as payback for earlier misdeeds.

"Are they living here in Dublin? I'd love to meet them. It seems only fair, now that you know my family."

"They'll be arriving tomorrow for the holiday," he said. "And I want all of you at my house tomorrow night. With a crowd so large, it will be a bit of a tight fit, but I want you to see how I live, get to know my family." He regarded her with a hopeful expression. "Do you think Megan can keep Mick in check for another evening?"

Nell laughed. "I'll see to it," she promised. "Let me check to see if anyone has made other plans for tomorrow, but you can count on me being there. I'm looking forward to it. Are you sure you wouldn't rather have a get-together at a pub or restaurant? There would be less to do."

"Trust me, I've managed a few gatherings this size and larger before, though generally not in my home. Thanks to my late wife, I have all of the best caterers on speed dial."

"And just when I was about to offer you my help," she teased.

"Your help would be welcome, of course," he said quickly. "No party is successful without a woman's touch."

"And Kiera won't mind me intruding?"

"Kiera will be on her knees giving thanks. She's all thumbs in a kitchen and when it comes to setting a buffet table, she considers it complete when the paper plates and plastic forks are piled at one end."

"Oh, dear," Nell said. "Perhaps I can give her a few gentle pointers."

Dillon laughed. "You can certainly try."

Inside the hotel lobby, he bent down and kissed her cheek. "Thank you for another remarkable evening, Nell, dear."

"Thank you," she said. "It was definitely memorable."

"That it was. I'll pick you up tomorrow afternoon at five. Tell the others to come at seven. Will that do?"

"That will do perfectly," she said. "I'll be looking forward to it."

Probably a whole lot more than any woman her age ought to be.

Matthew was happily engaged in a rather lengthy kiss with Laila outside her room when the elevator doors opened. He broke away just as his grandmother stepped into the hallway.

"Don't let me interrupt," she said, her eyes twinkling with amusement.

Still holding Laila's hand, Matthew frowned at Nell. "Are you just getting home? Everyone else got back a while ago."

"Dillon and I went for a walk," she said. "One of the best parts of any evening is the talk after of how things went."

"It is, isn't it?" Laila agreed. "And what conclusion did you reach?"

"That the lack of bloodshed was promising," Nell said with a laugh.

Laila chuckled with her, but Matthew was less amused. "Gram, are you really sure you know what you're doing?"

A door across the hall opened and Mick stepped out with Megan trying to hold him back. "I'd like to know the same," he said, a scowl in place.

Nell looked from her son to her grandson with her own scowl deepening. "I expected something like this from you, Mick, but you, as well, Matthew? That surprises me."

Not especially happy about being lumped in with his uncle, Matthew winced. "I'm just concerned."

"Well, there's no need to be. Now, before I go to my own room, I want to let you know that we're all invited to Dillon's home tomorrow to meet his daughter and grandchildren. I expect you to be there at seven. Moreover I expect you to remember your manners. Do I make myself clear?"

"Of course, Gram," Matthew said dutifully.

"Yes, Ma," Mick said, though he was clearly unhappy about it.

"I'll see to it," Megan promised, already tugging Mick back into their room and closing the door.

"As will I," Laila chimed in, following suit with Matthew.

Only after she'd closed the door did it apparently dawn on her what she'd done. She regarded Matthew with alarm.

"Do not get any ideas," she warned him. "I was just trying to help defuse the situation."

"Really?" Matthew said, glancing toward the king-size bed they were supposed to have been sharing on this trip. "One risky situation averted and now it appears there's another."

"Oh, no, there's not," Laila said firmly. "You can go now."

"That bed looks awfully comfortable," he commented.

"It is, but you're not testing it," she said, even as he sat on the edge and bounced up and down a couple of times. "Okay, fine. You've seen for yourself that it's a lovely bed. Now, go back to your own room."

He snagged her hand and pulled her down next to him. His gaze held hers. "Do you really want this opportunity to go to waste? It seems like a shame."

Her lips curved. "It is a shame, but that's the way it is. We took vows."

"It wasn't as if they were in a church or before a judge."

"A promise is a promise, Matthew." Her gaze narrowed. "Or are you admitting that yours mean nothing?"

He heaved a sigh. "Mine are serious and binding," he assured her. "Unless both parties agree to amend them."

"Well, both parties aren't agreeing, so go away."

"You're sure?"

"If I were sure and totally in my right mind, you'd never have gotten on this side of the door, but I'm trying very hard to do the right thing here. You could help me out."

There it was, that call for him to take the moral high ground. If he didn't do it, what kind of a man would that make him? An opportunistic one, at best. He reminded himself he was in this relationship for the long haul, not another quickie in the sack, no matter how incredible he knew it would be.

He stood reluctantly, her hand still in his. "You really are going to make a better man of me," he said, not entirely pleased by that at the moment.

To his surprise she looped her arms around his neck and kissed him gently. "You're already a good, honorable man," she told him quietly. "No need for improvement on my account."

If she'd declared her undying love for him, Matthew

couldn't have been more pleased. "You sounded as if you really meant that."

She smiled. "I really meant that. Now, go, before I forget all those resolutions I've made."

"I imagine I could make you forget all about them."

"I *know* you could," she said with a chuckle. "But then I'd have to take back everything I just said about you."

Ah, he thought, there was the rub.

"I'll see you in the morning," he said then. "Breakfast together at eight? It'll be almost like a morning after."

"After what?" she teased.

"Do not go down that path when I'm trying so hard to impress you with my restraint," he retorted. "Otherwise it'll be breakfast in bed with no apologies for what came before."

"I'll see you at eight in the dining room," she said quickly, a blush on her cheeks.

"That'll do," he said.

At least for now.

Laila made it to the hotel dining room before eight, only to find Trace, Abby and the girls already there.

"Join us," Trace said at once.

"Yes, please," Abby agreed. "We've hardly had a chance to talk since we arrived in Dublin."

From Laila's perspective that was probably a good thing, and she owed her stepnieces for that. She regarded them gratefully. "Have you been taking Mommy and Trace sightseeing?" she asked Carrie and Caitlyn.

"And shopping," Carrie said excitedly.

"I got lots and lots of new dresses," Caitlyn added. "They're for Christmas, but I think I'm getting other presents, too."

Laila laughed. "I imagine you will." It was a huge family, and everyone went a little crazy. There'd been pledges to cut back, agreement that the trip was gift enough for everyone, but not one person in the family believed such a thing applied to the children.

"So, sit," Trace said, standing to pull out a chair.

"I'm supposed to be meeting Matthew," she admitted.

"There's room for him, too," Abby said, shooting a warning glance at Trace, whose expression had darkened. "And here's my cousin now. Sit. Join us."

Matthew looked trapped. Laila knew exactly how he felt. She gave him a nothing-to-be-done shrug. They took the vacant seats and placed their order with the immediately attentive waiter.

"Having a good time in Ireland, Matthew?" Trace inquired politely, though his voice was cool.

"Excellent," Matthew responded stiffly.

Abby laughed. "What he really wants to know is whether you and *Laila* are having a good time," she said.

Laila jumped in. "We're both having a perfectly wonderful time. Now maybe we ought to change the subject."

The arrival of their food gave her time to study her sister-in-law's face. She thought she detected an unfamiliar glow. "Abby, you look particularly lovely. Do you happen to have some news you'd like to share?" she asked, approaching the topic of a possible pregnancy very carefully. She knew it had been a touchy subject between Abby and Trace.

Abby regarded her with shock, even as a grin spread across Trace's face.

"Told you we'd never get through the holidays without everyone figuring it out," he gloated.

Laila's eyes widened in delight. "Then I'm right? You're going to have a baby?"

Abby nodded, the blush in her cheeks deepening. "We are."

"Oh, that is so fabulous!" Laila said, knowing how much her brother had wanted this. He'd despaired of Abby ever being ready for another child. She jumped up to hug both of them.

"Congratulations!" Matthew told Trace, then kissed Abby. "You, too. We already know you make pretty good kids, even if they are little troublemakers."

"We are not troublemakers," Caitlyn protested. "We're angels. Grandpa Mick says so."

"Oh, what does he know?" Matthew teased.

"He knows *everything*," Carrie said loyally. "And we're going to be the best big sisters in the entire world."

"Unless it's a boy," Caitlyn amended. "I don't want a brother."

Abby shook her head at her attitude. "I'm afraid you'll have to take what we get."

"Couldn't we trade a boy in?" Caitlyn asked hopefully.

Laila looked across the table at her big brother. "There's certainly been a time or two when I wanted to do just that," she told them. "But in the end, brothers are pretty cool."

"Big brothers maybe," Carrie said, her expression thoughtful. "But little brothers are pests."

"Uncle Kevin and Uncle Connor are *my* little brothers, and they were pretty great when I was growing up," Abby told them. "Sure, they were pests sometimes, but not now."

Caitlyn frowned. "But that's a really long time to wait."

"Now that you mention it, it was," Abby said, smiling. "I guess you're just going to love this baby no matter what."

Listening to the exchange, Laila turned to study Matthew's reaction. To her surprise what she thought she saw on his face was wistfulness. She leaned closer.

"Everything okay?"

"Just having a moment," he said, with an obviously forced smile.

"What kind of moment?"

"How about we table this discussion for later?" he suggested, then turned to Trace. "What are you all up to today?"

"More shopping!" Carrie said with enthusiasm.

"I doubt we can squeeze another outfit into your suitcase," Trace said, though his expression was resigned. The whole family knew he was putty in the hands of his stepdaughters.

"Then we'll buy another suitcase," Caitlyn said with the cavalier attitude of someone who had never worried about airline luggage constraints.

"Well, buy something special to wear tonight," Laila told them, then grinned at Abby. "There's a party for the family at Dillon's house. We're *all* meeting his family this time."

"Oh, boy," Abby murmured. "Does Dad know?"

"He heard the same time we did, when Nell got back upstairs last night."

"How'd he take it?" Abby asked.

"Fortunately Megan was there to mediate before he said what he really thought," Laila told her. "He did agree to show up, though."

Matthew frowned at her, then turned to his cousin. "Abby, what do you really think of all this?"

"I think it's sweet, and I think wherever it leads is entirely up to Gram."

"Really?" he asked, his tone full of doubt.

"Really. None of us liked it one bit when she or anyone else meddled in our lives. We owe her the same courtesy. We need to back off and see how this plays out."

"What if it ends badly?"

"That's life, isn't it?" Abby said. "And we'll be there to support her, just as she'd be there for any one of us."

Laila rested her hand on Matthew's. "Abby's right, you know."

"I know," he said. "I just don't much like it. I feel as if we ought to try to save her or something."

"From falling in love with an old flame?" Laila asked. "It *is* sweet. I doubt she thinks she needs saving."

"Oh, what does she know," he grumbled, only to have all of the adults at the table laugh.

"You did not just say that," Abby teased. "I'm telling."

Matthew grimaced. "Don't you dare!"

"How are you going to stop me?"

"Want me to be the one who shares *your* news with the world?" he inquired.

Now it was Trace who chuckled. "I think he's effectively neutralized you, Abby."

"Afraid so," she admitted, then turned to Laila. "*You* could tell."

Laila held up her hands. "Not on your life. I'm Switzerland, one hundred percent neutral."

Matthew leaned in to give her a quick kiss. "And here I thought you were going to be loyal to me forever."

"Mostly, yes," she teased. "But it's not written in stone."

"She got you, Matthew," Caitlyn gloated.

Though it was clear the girls hadn't followed every word of the conversation, they had quick wits and were always eager to see any member of the family one-up someone else. Their loyalty was even more suspect.

"*Et tu, et tu,* little Brutuses?" Matthew asked with feigned despair.

"What does that mean?" Carrie asked.

"It means Matthew is a big baby," Abby declared, even as she regarded him with affection.

"And your mother is a big tease," he countered.

Laila looked from one to the other, then to her brother. "I love this family."

Trace smiled even as he warned, "Careful what you wish for, sis."

That was the thing, though. She thought she was finally starting to wish for blissful happiness, and it was the man seated next to her who was going to bring that into her life forever.

10

Matthew couldn't explain why he'd been so thrown by the news of Abby's pregnancy. Until recently he hadn't given much thought to having children. Oh, he'd always assumed he would marry and have them eventually, but until he'd fallen in love with Laila, it had been more theoretical. Even when they'd discussed the subject days earlier, the idea hadn't felt entirely real to him. He'd just been exploring the subject, testing his own idle thoughts against hers.

Suddenly this morning, sitting with his glowing cousin, her doting husband and those two little minxes from Abby's first marriage, he'd wanted what they had. He wanted it *now,* and, more than ever, he wanted it with Laila.

As he and Laila left the hotel after breakfast to go on their own shopping expedition, he fell silent, still thinking about his unexpected reaction.

They'd gone only a block when Laila steered him

toward the park across the street and found a bench bathed in sunshine. The morning air was chilly, but the warmth of the sun made it bearable.

"Sit," she commanded.

"Have I done something wrong?" he inquired lightly. "You've your mistress-of-the-classroom manner about you."

Laila smiled at that. "Sorry. I didn't mean to. You've just been distracted ever since we found out about Abby being pregnant. What's that about?"

He gave her a lingering, thoughtful look, wondering if she was really ready to hear what was on his mind. "You sure you want to know?"

"I wouldn't have asked if I didn't."

"Okay, then," he said, then held her gaze. "I was envisioning you carrying our child, your skin glowing the way Abby's was, me looking as thrilled and excited as Trace obviously is."

She blinked at the clearly unexpected response, then sat back, silent.

"Told you you'd find it disconcerting," he said.

"Oh, it is that," she said eventually, then met his gaze. "Strangely enough, I can see it, too. Ever since we discussed children, the idea of having a baby has been on my mind."

Her reply startled him. "Really?"

She nodded. "I have to admit, though, that having a little person dependent on me scares the living daylights out of me."

"Why?"

"What if I'm no good at being a mom?"

"You will be," he said with confidence. "What else worries you?"

"It implies a future we haven't come close to agreeing to."

"Matter of time," he said, again with absolute confidence.

She eyed him curiously. "Have you given this a lot of thought?"

"Only theoretically, to be honest. Then, just now, I was sitting there enjoying my eggs, and there it was, this longing to have a family—you, kids. Who knows, maybe even a dog. I had this whole image in my head. It felt real, Laila."

She smiled, though it didn't quite reach her eyes. "Were we in that house we discussed the other day?"

"Most definitely. The kids were on the beach, the dog was running in circles around them."

"And what were we doing?"

"Sitting on our porch with our morning cups of coffee, enjoying it all," he said. "I felt a hundred percent content."

"Any idea how I was feeling?"

He smiled at the curiosity behind the question. "You looked happy." He studied her face. "How do you think you'd feel?"

"I suppose I never let myself think that far ahead."

"Because of our situation?"

"No, not just with you, with anyone. Things were never that serious that I allowed myself to look too far into the future. I was too afraid of building up my hopes, only to be disappointed. You've had legions of women in your life, Matthew. I've dated, but until you, only one person came close to becoming important."

"The guy you've said bored you silly?"

"That's the one."

"But you do like kids, right?" he asked, surprisingly anxious to know if they were at least on the same page about that. Otherwise it would throw a huge wrinkle in his plans. Was it a deal breaker, though, if she didn't? He couldn't be sure.

She smiled. "With Carrie, Caitlyn and all those other darling little O'Brien rug rats underfoot, how could I not? You guys make great babies."

"Can't argue with you there," he said, relieved.

She gave him a long look. "So, this image of yours didn't panic you?"

He shook his head. "Not a bit."

She nodded slowly. "Good to know."

"Laila?"

"Yes?"

"Fair warning," he said, leveling a look directly into her eyes. "I'm going to do everything in my power to make sure it happens."

She seemed a little taken aback by the certainty of his declaration, but she didn't get up and take off. He considered that promising. Very, very promising.

Laila managed to stay outwardly calm during the rest of her morning with Matthew, but full-blown panic set in the minute she was alone in her hotel room. She called Jess and Connie.

"Bar in ten minutes," she said to each of them. Neither one argued. Obviously her tone had communicated her state of mind.

As she sat at a corner table and waited for them, she tried to go over what she'd found most worrisome in that whole exchange with Matthew. She still hadn't figured it out when Jess arrived, looking harried, her hair damp.

"You caught me just out of the shower," she said. "I didn't want to take the time to blow-dry my hair, so if I wind up with pneumonia, it's on you."

Laila laughed. "It wasn't quite that urgent."

"Well, you sounded distraught. What's Matthew done now?"

Laila frowned at the question. Was she so predictable that all her crises these days were Matthew-related? "Why do you assume it has anything to do with Matthew?"

Jess rolled her eyes. "Sadly, panic is almost always related to a man."

"Isn't that the truth?" Connie agreed, joining them.

Laila sighed. "I need a drink."

"First backup from us, now a drink," Connie said. "It's definitely about Matthew."

Laila wondered why she'd thought they'd be any help at all. They were O'Briens, after all, albeit Connie had married into the family, and fairly recently at that.

"She's regretting calling us," Jess said with a grin.

"I am," Laila agreed.

"When the problem's with an O'Brien, who better to talk you through it?" Jess said. "Except maybe my husband the shrink. Want me to get Will down here? He was a little disappointed not to be invited."

"Men, even shrinks, are not what I need around right now," Laila replied.

Jess called over the waiter, ordered a bottle of white wine, then looked at Laila and waited.

"I think she expects you to start talking," Connie prodded.

Laila knew she couldn't reveal how the subject of babies and kids had come up, so she finally said simply, "He's talking about children."

Both of her friends regarded her blankly.

"I'm not seeing the problem," Jess said.

Connie laughed. "I am. Laila hasn't quite wrapped her head around the idea of a relationship, and now Matthew's taken a giant leap forward. I felt the same way when Thomas raised the subject again just after we talked about it the other day. It came up out of the blue that very same night. Is this some family hot topic these days?"

"Could be," Laila replied, careful to keep her tone neutral. "So, are you seriously considering it now? Jenny's just gone off to college. You're finally free to do whatever you want."

"I think what I want is to have a baby with Thomas," she admitted, her eyes sparkling. "Truthfully, we haven't been doing anything to prevent it, if you know what I mean. I figured I was past the point of worrying about getting pregnant."

"So, even before Thomas brought up the subject, you could have gotten pregnant?" Laila asked. "The risk was a pretty big thing to ignore, wasn't it?"

"I figured I'd leave it in God's hands," Connie said defensively. Her cheeks turned pink. "But ever since the subject came up the other day, we've been trying." She grinned. "A lot."

Jess chuckled. "Lucky you."

"The process definitely has its perks," Connie agreed, then gestured toward her untouched glass of wine. "Which is why I'm not drinking that," she added sadly. "But let's focus on Laila's issue. Do you want to have kids?"

"Sure, sometime," Laila said.

"With Matthew?" Jess asked.

"There's nobody else in my life," she responded.

"That wasn't really the question," Jess said impatiently. "When the prospect of a family comes to mind, do you see Matthew in the picture?"

She gave the question some thought, tried to see that image Matthew himself had described earlier, then nodded. "Yeah, I do. Is that insane, or what? Do you really think he's Dad material?"

"I do, and it would only be insane if you didn't love him," Connie said. "Since you do, it makes perfect sense to me."

"Agreed," Jess said.

"Neither of you even batted an eye just then," Laila said. "Are you that sure I'm in love with Matthew and that he loves me?"

"Looks that way from where I'm sitting," Jess said.

"Me, too," Connie added. "Why do you still have doubts? Is it because of this whole mess with your father?"

"I suppose that's part of it," Laila conceded. "Even though he drives me insane, he *is* still my father. I've always respected him, and he seems a hundred percent certain that what's going on with me and Matthew is wrong."

"Maybe that's because you acted as if it were," Jess reminded her gently.

"The whole secrecy thing," Laila concluded.

"It was definitely a mistake," Connie told her. "Thomas and I tried the same thing, but fortunately a few people caught on to what was happening and dragged us out of the closet. Ironically, Mick's the one we really have to thank for that. He insisted Thomas not treat our relationship as if it were something to be ashamed of. Right after that we got Nell's blessing, and that was that."

"I suppose letting my parents be the last to know didn't help, either," Laila said, then waved off the topic. "Too late to change any of that now."

"If your father's blessing matters that much to you, you could always go to him and lay your cards on the table. Tell him you and Matthew are in love, that it's serious. I think that's what Will would advise," Jess said. "He's very big on full disclosure."

Laila nodded slowly. "I'll think about it." The truth was, though, that she wasn't sure she wanted to count on anything from her father anymore. Ignoring him seemed like the only way to move forward with her life. She had no idea if that was childish, or if it was the only rational, mature way to deal with the reality of his disparaging view of her. Oh, he loved her in his fashion. She simply didn't measure up in his eyes to the son and heir he'd wanted to take over the bank.

Jess took a sip of her wine, studying Laila over the rim of her glass. "So you and Matthew with kids, huh?"

"It's far from a done deal," Laila said quickly.

Connie and Jess exchanged an amused look.

"That's what you think," Connie said.

Jess nodded agreement. "Don't you know by now that O'Briens always get what they want?"

Laila's heart skipped a beat or two at the realization that they were exactly right. And what Matthew clearly wanted was her *and* a family.

"Good girl-talk?" Matthew inquired with an amused look when he picked Laila up in her room to go to Dillon O'Malley's for dinner.

Laila frowned at the question. "How do you know about that?"

"Will told Mack he was having a perfectly wonderful afternoon with his wife when you called and Jess went running off to meet you in the bar. She came back a little tipsy, by the way. Mack mentioned to Susie that there was some kind of crisis and Jess and Connie were called in. Susie asked me what was going on." He shrugged. "The usual grapevine."

"I knew this was a bad idea," she grumbled in an undertone.

"What?"

"Getting any more involved with an O'Brien. One of you is enough trouble. Together, you're beyond daunting."

"I can have them all back off," Matthew offered. "Of course, you were the one who sent out the distress call today. What was it about, anyway?"

"Doesn't really matter," she said.

"Was it what we talked about this morning?" he persisted. "The whole kid thing?"

She seemed reluctant to answer, but she finally nodded. "The implication of the whole kid thing."

"But you're in a better place now? No more panic?"

She laughed. "I wouldn't go that far. Could we not talk about this right now? Let's just focus on being supportive of Nell tonight. Aren't you curious to see Dillon O'Malley's home and to meet his family?"

"Not half as curious as Mick is. When he found out Nell was going over there at five, he wanted to follow her instead of waiting till seven like the rest of us."

"Megan stopped him, I assume."

"Not without a struggle. I believe Jeff and Thomas had to rush in and provide a little muscle."

Laila stared at him. "Are you serious?"

"You know Mick. What do you think?"

She shook her head. "It's promising to be quite an evening."

"That it is," Matthew said. "We could skip it."

"Not on your life. If there are fireworks, I want to be there."

"By the way, I told Luke he could ride over with us. Is that okay with you? He's feeling like a bit of an outsider since everyone else in the family is paired off at the moment."

"It's fine with me. Where is he?"

"I sent him ahead to get a taxi. He should be waiting for us out front."

Laila gave him a chiding look. "Why didn't you say something sooner? I've been dawdling as if we had all the time in the world."

"We do," Matthew said. "Believe me, I'd rather be right here in this room with you than over there for the inquisition."

She gave him a look of disgust. "It's not going to be like that. We'll see to it."

"You have a lot more faith in our skills at mediation than I do," he said as he followed her from the room.

Outside they found Luke waiting with a taxi, looking as unexcited about the evening's prospects as Matthew felt.

"I still say we should have the driver drop us at a pub," Luke said. "I even spotted a busy Italian restaurant over by Trinity College earlier. It was packed with people our age. You could smell the garlic and tomato sauce clear out on the street."

"Not on your life," Laila protested. "Give the driver Dillon's address."

The taxi took them to a nearby suburb with lush, if small, lawns and impressive houses. Matthew whistled.

"This place should allay some of Mick's fears," Matthew said. "It's quite a few steps above a hovel. Obviously Dillon's done well for himself."

"Who knew a little tobacco shop could do this well?" Luke added.

"Dillon has a few other businesses," Laila told them. "Which you would know if either of you had bothered to talk to him."

Matthew regarded her with surprise. "What sort of businesses?"

"There are a few more tobacco shops in outlying villages," she told him. "A wee bit of landscaping, as he put it, but I gathered it's a whole lot more than that.

In fact he and Jake have a lot in common. They were talking about it at the pub last night."

Matthew shook his head. "There goes Mick's last hope that the man was after Gram's money."

As soon as they rang the doorbell, it was opened by a young Irish woman about Luke's age with a peaches-and-cream complexion, black hair and blue eyes that snapped with anger.

"You must be some of the visiting Americans," she said. "Here to bring joy to the holidays."

Matthew swallowed a chuckle, then noticed that Luke was studying her with evident fascination.

"You don't seem all that happy to see us," Luke commented. "And why is that? We're harmless enough."

"Moira, why are our guests still standing outside?" Dillon boomed, giving what had to be his granddaughter a chiding look. "That's no way to treat company."

"They're your company, not mine," she retorted.

Dillon shook his head as she walked away without an apology or a backward glance. He invited them into a large foyer that featured boughs of richly scented evergreen entwined with lights along the rails of a wide staircase. A large Waterford crystal bowl sat on a center table and was filled with lavish sprigs of holly and shining red Christmas balls.

While Matthew took in their surroundings, he noted that his brother's gaze had followed Moira.

"Charming girl," Luke said and actually seemed to mean it.

Dillon merely shook his head. "My granddaughter, Moira. She's not happy about being here. In fact, as near as I can tell, she's not happy about anything these days. Either that or she's simply intent on seeing the rest of us miserable."

"Perhaps I can coax her out of her mood," Luke offered eagerly.

He handed his coat to Matthew, then went off in the direction Moira had taken, disappearing into what was apparently a living room with a large Christmas tree that twinkled with white lights and more decorations than Matthew had ever seen before. For a widower Dillon had taken great care with seeing that his home was festive. Matthew couldn't help wondering if that was for his grandmother's benefit, or just family tradition.

Dillon's troubled gaze followed Luke. "I don't hold out much hope for his success with cheering my granddaughter."

"Oh, Luke has a way with women," Matthew assured him. "Moira seems to present exactly the sort of challenge he's been missing on this trip."

"Has anyone else arrived?" Laila asked.

"Only Nell's here so far. She's in the kitchen trying to give my daughter, Kiera, a few pointers on entertaining a crowd of this size." He shook his head, his expression gloomy. "That's not going so well, either."

Laila laughed. "I'll see what I can do. Matthew, are you coming with me?"

"Maybe I should check on Luke."

"Has your brother ever wanted or needed your help with a woman?" she asked.

"You have a point. Dillon, what else can I do?"

"You can help me get the bar ready, if you wouldn't mind."

Matthew nodded. "I'd be happy to."

Matthew cast a look after Laila as she went in the direction Dillon had pointed out to her, then turned to their host. "It was very generous of you to invite all of us to your home. Are you sure it was a good idea?"

Dillon laughed. "I knew it would make Nell happy, and I wanted her to meet my family. I swear, though, they seem intent on making yours look downright welcoming by comparison. Moira's sullen, Kiera's rude and my grandsons have taken off for who knows where. Quite likely the pub down the street. I have no idea what Nell must think of us."

"No one understands twisted family dynamics better than the O'Briens," Matthew said, taking pity on him. "Gram won't hold their behavior against you." He gave the older man a sly look. "She seems quite taken with you."

Dillon regarded him with amusement. "Are you asking whether my intentions are honorable, young man?"

Matthew shrugged. "I don't have a lot of practice at that sort of thing, but I suppose I am."

"My intentions were honorable enough to suit Nell's grandfather when he allowed me to see her all those years ago, and they are now."

"But you live in Dublin and Gram's life is across the ocean now," Matthew reminded him. "How do you intend to work that out?"

"You're a step or two ahead of us," Dillon said. "But if decisions need to be made, I assure you your grandmother and I are capable of making the ones that are right for us."

Matthew understood that Dillon was warning him

off, but he couldn't help asking, "But you do foresee some kind of a future with her?"

Dillon smiled. "Some kind? Yes. It could be nothing more than a rekindled friendship with shared memories, or something more. As I said before, Matthew, we haven't defined it, haven't even discussed it for that matter. We're content to be living in the moment. There's a lesson to be had in that, I think."

"And here all I can think about is the future," Matthew countered.

"Because you're young enough to have a long, open road spread out ahead of you," Dillon said mildly. "Nell and I are at the end of ours. Neither of us knows what tomorrow could bring. Today is what we have. We'll make the very best of it."

He held Matthew's gaze with a directness Matthew couldn't help appreciating, then added, "And we'll do it thoughtfully."

Matthew smiled at his clear-eyed view of the situation and the carefully disguised hint of censure in his voice.

"For whatever it's worth, you have my blessing," he told Dillon. "You still have a sales job to do with my uncle Mick."

"Believe me, I'm well aware that he's going to be a hard sell," Dillon told him. "But when it comes down to it, Nell's approval is the one that counts the most. If I can make her truly happy, then I trust that she raised the kind of family that will be glad for her."

They'd just managed to put the bottles of wine and whiskey out, along with an impressive variety of obviously expensive crystal glasses, when Moira came storming past, a scowl on her face.

"That man is impossible," she declared, grabbing a coat off a peg in the hallway. "I'm out of here."

"To go where?" Dillon demanded.

"Anywhere he isn't," she said, her heated gaze warning Luke to stay behind. The door slammed behind her.

"That obviously went well," Matthew said, laughing.

Luke had the genuinely bewildered look of a man not used to rejection. "I think she actually hates me," he said.

Dillon's laughter joined Matthew's. "Son, she hasn't singled you out. Our Moira hates everyone today, and I've no idea why."

Luke's expression turned determined. "Well, I intend to find out."

Matthew moved to stop him. "Don't you think you should stay out of it? The two of you have barely met and it hasn't gone well so far. Besides, the rest of the family will be here soon."

"Oh, I'll be back before dinner's served," Luke said, sounding grimly sure of himself. He gave Dillon a weak smile. "Hopefully in one piece and with Moira in tow."

"I wish you luck," Dillon said, then watched him leave. "Is he the kind of man who needs a bit of challenge in his life?" he asked Matthew.

"Seems that way. He hasn't had nearly enough of them."

"Well, if that's what he's after, he'll not do better than Moira. She's been turning her mother's hair gray for years, and I've considered tearing mine out over her."

Matthew chuckled. "Then they're well suited," Matthew assured him.

It was already turning out to be quite an eventful evening, and Mick had yet to put in an appearance.

11

Nell thought she'd been demonstrating great restraint with Kiera. Because Kiera was Dillon's daughter and this had once been her home, Nell took deliberate care not to lay claim to the kitchen and take over the dinner preparations. Her efforts at diplomacy were wasted.

She told herself Kiera's obvious resentment of every carefully phrased suggestion was understandable. She'd come here expecting a traditional family holiday, and now she was about to be surrounded by strangers, one of whom shared a past with her father. It must be terribly disconcerting to discover her father had a history with someone other than her mother, a history she'd not even known about. Nell understood because Mick, Thomas and Jeff were struggling with the same knowledge in their own ways.

"I'm sorry that tonight's dinner has overburdened you," she said, trying yet again to reach out to the unhappily divorced woman who was only in her late forties, but looked older. "I'm willing to help with whatever needs to be done."

"It's my father's house," Kiera responded ungraciously. "He can invite anyone he likes here."

"But you'd been expecting a family holiday, I'm sure. And now you've all these visitors descending on you."

Kiera was silent for a moment, then admitted, "To be honest, it takes some of the pressure off, you know. My father and I haven't always been close. We reconciled for my mother's sake before she died." She gave Nell a resigned look. "I imagine he told you that. It's his way of letting people know not to expect a joyous family gathering."

"He mentioned there had been some distance between you at one time," Nell admitted. "He believes you're closer now. At least, he wants that to be true."

Kiera shrugged. "If the occasional holiday meal counts, then we are, but we'll never be the traditional warm and fuzzy family."

Nell laughed. "Few families are, at least all of the time. Believe me, we've had our differences in mine. My sons, who'll be here tonight, were barely speaking for years. The holiday meals, which I insisted we all share, and the Sunday dinners were quite tense."

Kiera looked vaguely intrigued by that. "Then why bother? Would it not have been less stressful to leave them be?"

"Less stressful, of course," Nell agreed. "But in the end, family is the most important thing we have. These are the people with whom we share a history, the ones who'll be there when needed without question."

"Seriously?" Kiera said. "That seems to me to put

an optimistic spin on things. My father wasn't always there for me."

"Did you give him the opportunity?" Nell asked gently. "Most of us won't go where we're unwelcome, family or not. Most of us can only have the door slammed in our faces so many times before we give up."

Kiera sighed. "I suppose you're right. I did shut him out—literally and figuratively—more than once."

"But that door is open now," Nell pointed out. "Make whatever effort it requires to keep it that way. I know it's what your father wants. His whole face lights up when he talks of you and your children."

Kiera gave her a rueful look. "Even Moira? There are days when even I don't like her much. I should be ashamed to say such a thing about my own child, but it's true."

Nell laughed. "She'll grow out of it. You did, didn't you?"

After a startled pause, Kiera laughed. "You're not the first to draw the comparison, and it's true. I suppose I did." She looked around the kitchen, which was littered with boxes of food left by a caterer. She appeared surprisingly daunted.

"I've no idea what to do with this," she confided. "I've never managed a meal for so many before, not even when the cooking has been done by someone else."

"Do you have serving dishes?" Nell inquired, seeing an opening to take charge as she'd been longing to do.

"Cupboards full of them," Kiera told her.

"Okay, then," Nell said decisively. "We'll need several platters, a half dozen large bowls."

"Now, those I can find," Kiera said, obviously relieved to have someone knowledgeable take over.

They worked in companionable silence transferring the abundance of food to serving dishes. When Laila joined them, they started carrying everything into the dining room to a buffet table that had been set up along one wall. Fine china and silver had been laid out at one end and the long table had been covered with an exquisite antique cloth trimmed in Irish lace. Candles of every size lit the room with a soft glow.

"It's going to be lovely in here," Nell said appreciatively. "There will be room enough for all of us with some to spare."

"When I was small, my parents had dinner parties often," Kiera said, her expression suddenly nostalgic. "I used to sit on the stairs and listen to all the talk and laughter drifting out of this room and wonder what it would be like to host such a party."

Nell patted her arm. "Well, now you know. It's a bit chaotic, but the result will be well worth it. The key to successful entertaining is not allowing yourself to be intimidated. Take a deep, calming breath before the guests arrive."

Kiera gave her a pointed look. "Too late for that. Some of you are already here."

Nell chuckled. "Ah, but you've made me and Laila your helpers now. You've the two of us as backup."

"But I've done none of the cooking," Kiera said, looking over the steaming food.

"You've created a welcoming atmosphere," Nell corrected. "The food is secondary."

She noticed Laila gave her a surprised look and knew

she was thinking of what a point Nell made at home to provide home-cooked meals for these family celebrations. At her warning glance, though, Laila said nothing.

Nell listened to the sounds of conversation and even the occasional laugh coming from the living room. "It seems peaceful enough in there. Shall we get everyone in here for the meal before there's trouble?"

Kiera regarded her curiously. "What sort of trouble?"

"My sons aren't sure they approve of me spending time with your father. One of them is particularly outspoken about it, though I've warned him to mind his manners tonight."

Kiera uttered a genuine, unfettered laugh for the first time since they'd met. "Then it truly isn't just my father and me who've difficulties from time to time. I thought perhaps you were saying those things before just to be kind."

"Oh, no," Nell assured her. "You'll see for yourself before the night is over, I'm sure."

"Then this is an evening I can look forward to, after all," Kiera said. "Now, if only my Moira doesn't spoil it with another of her rebellions."

Laila gave her a sympathetic look. "I doubt you need to worry about that. Nell's grandson has that situation in hand."

Nell regarded Laila with surprise, quickly deducing which grandson was likely to have taken on Kiera's troublesome daughter. She'd seen for herself just how beautiful Moira was.

"Luke, I imagine," she said, knowing he was the one who would have been unable to resist such a challenge.

Laila nodded. "Of course."

Nell smiled. That was a turn of events she definitely hadn't anticipated, but she couldn't deny it was a welcome one. She'd worried about Luke for a while now, seen how restless and unhappy he was now that everyone else seemed to be settled—or nearly so, she amended, thinking of Matthew and Laila.

Though she'd been scandalized when Luke had brought Mack's ex-girlfriend, Kristen Lewis, into Mick's home, she'd never once voiced an objection. Still, she'd seen it for the trouble it was likely to cause. Susie would never make peace with having that woman as a member of the family. No amount of time or mediation was likely to change that.

She recalled her two-minute introduction to the challenging Moira and thought there was just the right amount of fire there to keep Luke fascinated, perhaps even enough to distract him from the problematic Kristen.

"Kiera, why don't I go with you to make the introductions to my family," Nell suggested. "Laila, you go ahead and remind them to be civilized."

Laila chuckled. "Now, what are the odds of my word meaning a thing?"

Nell laughed with her. "Then you'll see that Matthew behaves. I'll handle the rest."

And she would keep a close eye on Luke and Moira while she was at it. Wouldn't it be a lovely thing to leave Ireland with both of her grandsons' futures assured?

Laila closed her eyes and settled against Matthew's side on the taxi ride back to the hotel, his arm around her shoulders.

"It turned out to be a wonderful evening, after all, didn't it?" she murmured. "Nell has a way of putting people at ease and keeping the conversation flowing. Even Mick eventually relaxed and stopped his scowling."

"Don't think he's been won over just yet," Matthew warned. "I heard talk of him hiring a private investigator."

"Not to look into Dillon's background?" Laila said, sitting up to give him a shocked look. "Surely Mick no longer thinks Dillon is some sort of schemer where Nell's concerned."

"Oh, no," Matthew said, a smile on his lips. "Now he's convinced the man is living on some kind of ill-gotten gains."

"Oh, for heaven's sake," Laila said. "I know he's just being protective, but isn't that a little far-fetched?"

"I'd say so," Matthew agreed, then regarded her thoughtfully. "Is it really so different from the way your father looks at me, as if I'm about to ruin his daughter's life?"

"Totally different circumstances," Laila insisted.

"Is it really?"

"Matthew, he's not really worried about me," she said with conviction. "He's worried only about his precious bank's reputation."

"I'm just saying that, perhaps in his mind, it's the same thing."

She regarded Matthew curiously. "Why are you suggesting this now?"

"Listening to Mick tonight gave me a different perspective on protectiveness, for one thing," he said. "For another, I still hate being the cause of this rift between you and your parents. I'd be happy to find a new spin that might allow you to make peace with them. I don't want to be the reason they're not in your life."

"It's not up to you to broker peace," Laila said. "I doubt it's even possible. I think things have gone too far this time."

"You still breathing?" Matthew inquired.

She studied him with a furrowed gaze. "What's your point?"

"As long as you're all still here on earth, there's always a way to fix things." His expression sobered. "Don't wait too long, Laila. It will only get harder and harder to swallow your pride."

"I've no intention of swallowing my pride," she said, knowing she sounded as stubborn as any O'Brien. "I've done it my whole life, tried to mold myself into the daughter my father would respect. No more. Let him swallow his this time."

"Didn't he do that by calling?" Matthew suggested.

She sighed at the memory of that terse message. There was no denying it had been an overture, particularly when combined with Trace's revelation that her father was having second thoughts about letting her go from the bank.

"I suppose," she conceded reluctantly.

"Maybe you should call him. It'll be Christmas day after tomorrow. I'm sure your parents would love to hear from you. I imagine it's the greatest gift you could give them this holiday season."

She frowned at him. "When did you start worrying about my parents' feelings?"

"I'm not," he said. "It's yours I care about. And, no matter how you deny it, I know you'll not be happy until this whole mess has been resolved, and you're all at least on speaking terms again."

"Isn't it enough that you and I are speaking again?" she asked wistfully, knowing he was right about the need to mend fences with her family. She just wasn't ready yet to take the steps necessary to do it.

Matthew chuckled and pulled her closer. "Indeed, things seem to be working out very well for me recently. Maybe that's why I want to see the whole world happy and on an even keel again. I've even become a big booster of Gram and Dillon and, though I think it's likely he's lost his mind, I could summon up some enthusiasm for Luke and the insufferable Moira, as well."

"Now, that one's a stretch even for me," Laila said with a laugh. "Serves him right, though, to be falling for an impossible woman. She's just what he deserves. Where is Luke, by the way? Why didn't he ride back with us?"

"He claimed he wanted to give us some privacy," Matthew said. "And that he wanted to help with the cleanup at the house."

Laila stared at him, openmouthed with shock. "Now you're just making up stories. Luke is washing dishes and throwing out the trash?"

"Last time I saw him, he was," Matthew confirmed. "With Moira grumbling at him the whole time about how badly he was doing it." He grinned. "She did seem to have a bit of a twinkle in her eyes when she said it, though. Perhaps there's hope after all that she'll turn out to be a lovely woman."

"Hopes and dreams are beautiful things," Laila agreed, then grinned. "Then there's pure fantasy."

"Well, I'm just happy that Luke's fantasy kept him at Dillon's, so you and I can be alone."

Laila regarded him with amusement. "Have I reduced you to being content with a few stolen moments of privacy in a taxi?"

"I was thinking more of the time we could spend together at the hotel without my brother waiting up to offer his thoughts on my comings and goings."

"Luke's been keeping track of you?"

"He has," Matthew confirmed. "It amuses him that you've sent me back to my lonely bed every night since we arrived."

"We agreed," she reminded him.

"Is this one of those promises that people regret the minute they're uttered?" he inquired, his expression hopeful. "It certainly is for me." He studied her. "How about you? Any second thoughts?"

"A ton of them," she confessed.

His expression brightened. "Well, then…"

"Don't be getting any ideas, Matthew O'Brien. You were right to suggest this time-out from sex. It's been a revelation."

"In what way?"

"We haven't been bored to tears."

He smiled. "Were you thinking we would be?"

"To be honest, I wasn't sure." She gave him a pleased look. "You actually went shopping with me and hardly grumbled about it. I never expected that."

"Well, don't be thinking that it's likely to happen on a regular basis," he said with an exaggerated shudder. "Women shop. Men buy. It's a whole different experience."

"In what way?"

"It takes a lot less time."

She nodded. She could see his point. Truthfully, she could buy all of her Christmas gifts in one whirlwind expedition most of the time. There'd been something about shopping here, though, that was different. She'd wanted each gift to be memorable and meaningful, and there'd been so much to choose from. And she'd had to select one thing for herself, a lasting reminder of the trip. In the end she'd chosen a pair of Waterford crystal champagne flutes, hoping they'd someday find a purpose at anniversary celebrations. She'd smiled even as she'd signed the outrageously high credit card slip.

"Well, you get points for tolerating it, anyway," she told him. "And for being so supportive of Nell and Dillon. I think for the longest time I insisted on thinking of you as this shallow playboy."

At his hurt expression, she touched his cheek. "Sorry, but I did. Thinking of you any other way would have been too terrifying. I'd have had to consider the possibility that I could fall in love with you."

His eyes brightened. "Is that so? And now?"

She hesitated, reluctant to say the words aloud even now. Still, he deserved to hear them. "And now, I have," she said quietly.

"Have what?" he prodded, a twinkle in his eyes.

"You're going to make me say it, aren't you?"

"I am."

She drew in a deep breath, met his gaze, then said, "I've fallen in love with you."

At her words, Matthew let out a whoop of undisguised joy that had the taxi driver hitting the brakes and turning around.

"Sorry," Matthew said. "She just admitted she loved me."

The man gave him a smile, then once again eased forward in the traffic.

"I heard," he told them, glancing briefly into the rearview mirror. "One of the best parts of this job is hearing such a thing from time to time."

He made the tricky turn around the corner and pulled to a stop. "Now here you are at your hotel. Enjoy the rest of your evening. Happy Christmas to you, too."

"And to you," Laila said, exiting the cab and walking swiftly into the hotel lobby.

Matthew caught up with her in front of the elevators. "You in a hurry?"

"No, but I thought maybe you would be." She held his gaze and asked solemnly, "Do you want to come to my room with me?"

He gave her a long, lingering look. "You have no idea how badly I want exactly that," he said with undisguised emotion.

She frowned at what he didn't say. "But it's not going to happen, is it?"

"Not tonight," he said with regret.

"Because?"

"Because the next time we sleep together, Laila, I intend it to be our wedding night."

She heard the words as if they'd been spoken in a foreign tongue. The heartfelt tone registered, but not the meaning.

"Wedding night?" she echoed, her heart hammering.

He nodded. "That's the deal."

"You said earlier that you regretted our deal. I've agreed with you, invited you to my room, and you're turning me down?"

"I am," he said solemnly.

"Is this some kind of weird extortion?" she asked. "If I ever want sex with you again, I have to marry you?"

He laughed. "Something like that, though there's no proposal currently on the table."

She frowned at him. "You're not still thinking you'll convince me to marry you before we leave Ireland, are you?"

"I guess you'll have to wait and see," he said. "The anticipation will make the next few days that much more interesting, won't it?"

"I take back everything I said earlier about you being the kind of mature man I could envision falling in love with," she groused.

"Too late. And you didn't say you could envision a time when you might fall in love with me. You said you're *already* in love with me. I have the taxi driver as a witness."

"Did you get his name?" she taunted.

He laughed. "No, but I guarantee you I could find him again. Uncle Mick probably has that investigator of his on speed dial by now."

Not for the first time, Laila wondered if she could possibly be in her right mind to be in love with an O'Brien. And, despite her attempt to deny it, she *was* in love with him. The only thing still in doubt was what she—and he—intended to do about it.

Matthew decided it was best to let Laila stew for a while over the conversation they'd had the night before.

His declaration about waiting for a wedding night to sleep with her again had clearly rattled her. He liked seeing that quick rise of color in her cheeks and the vulnerability in her eyes. As strong as she was, he liked having the power to shake her up. She needed that from him, needed the unpredictability and passion and caring that underscored their relationship.

He was leaving the hotel to go for a walk and work off some restless energy when Trace appeared with a scowl on his face.

"My sister looks a little ragged and upset this morning," he noted. "She didn't look that way when we left Dillon's last night. Are you to blame?"

"More than likely," Matthew said readily, then chuckled. "Before you slug me, you might want to know it's because the subject of weddings came up."

Trace stared hard at him. "You proposed?"

"Not yet," he admitted. "That's on tonight's agenda, after church." He held his future brother-in-law's gaze. "Unless you object."

"Seriously?" Trace said, looking thoroughly taken aback, as if he'd never expected such a thought to cross Matthew's mind. "You really want Laila to marry you?"

"I have for a long time. I think she's finally warming to the idea."

"And yet today she looks completely out of sorts because the subject came up in some general sort of way?" Trace said. "I have to admit I'm confused."

"You had to be there, and some of the conversation isn't meant for your ears. It falls into the too-much-information category."

"Since I'm the one who's here, I suppose that leaves

me to ask the kind of questions my father would ask," Trace said.

Matthew gave him a rueful look. "Really? Couldn't we just skip those?"

Trace shrugged, apparently easily swayed from that unwanted duty. "I suppose the only thing that matters is whether Laila thinks you can make her happy."

Matthew gave him a solemn look. "And I can swear to you that I will do everything in my power to see that she is. I can provide for her. We'll have a home on the bay next door to Susie and Mack. It'll be designed and built exactly the way Laila wants it done. We'll fill it with kids."

Again, Trace looked stunned. "You've actually talked about having children?"

"Thanks to the big announcement that you and Abby haven't yet shared with the others, we have. I realized that morning at breakfast just how badly I want the whole family thing, and I want it with your sister. She's finally on the same page."

Trace looked doubtful. "You sure about that? There's still the situation with our father. I think that needs to be resolved, or she'll never be truly happy."

"I agree," Matthew said. "Which is why, if she agrees to marry me when I ask her tonight, I intend to do everything in my power to get them over here for the wedding." He gave Trace a sly look. "You could help with that."

Trace looked as if his head were reeling. "You want to get married here? In Ireland? And you want to do it before we go home?"

Matthew nodded. "I do."

Trace shook his head. "I definitely didn't see that coming."

"I don't know why," Matthew told him. "Half the family's been scheming for a while now. Gram's been the leader of the pack. I think she already has the special license locked in the safe in her room and a priest on standby. She probably started making calls to put things in motion before we ever left Chesapeake Shores. Once Gram senses there's romance in the air, there's nothing she won't do to see that it leads down the aisle."

"And Laila knows about this?"

Matthew nodded. "She had a bit of a meltdown when she first found out, but I think she's coming around now. The only thing she doesn't know for sure is when I intend to make it official with a ring. That has her a little on edge."

"Thus the harried state I caught her in," Trace deduced.

"Exactly."

"Laila's never been much for surprises," Trace warned him. "Mom tried to throw her a surprise birthday party once, but Laila found out about it. She was so embarrassed, she took off and no one could find her."

"She's not going to run away from this," Matthew said with confidence. He frowned. "At least I don't think she will. And lately she's started to enjoy being unpredictable and a little reckless."

"Not that I'm objecting, because I think it's exactly what she needs," Trace said. "But you do know those traits are precisely why my father objects so vehemently to you being in her life, right?"

"Do you think that will keep him from coming to the wedding?" Matthew asked.

Trace hesitated, then seemed to come to a decision. "Make your plans with my sister and leave the rest to me. I'll get my parents over here," he said with determination. "I learned manipulation from a couple of masters—my father and Mick."

"Gram's no slouch either," Matthew reminded him. "She'll be your backup if you need it. I imagine she could be persuaded to give a blistering lecture that even Lawrence Riley couldn't ignore."

"I'd actually love to hear that, but I doubt I'll need her," Trace said, then grinned conspiratorially. "I have the grandchild my parents have been longing for on the way. If they ever hope to see that baby, they'll be here and there will be smiles on their faces."

Matthew regarded Trace with new respect. "The O'Briens are definitely rubbing off on you," he said approvingly.

Trace nodded. "It'd be impossible for you not to. I'm married to the best one of the whole lot of you."

Matthew chuckled. "Does Abby understand what a hold she has on you?"

Trace gave him a resigned look. "She's known that since we were kids. It's a curse."

"Seems more like a blessing to me."

"There are days I see it that way, too." Trace gave him a knowing look. "Word of advice from someone who's been married a few years now?"

"Sure."

"Marriage is a tricky business, Matthew. Not every day will be perfect or what you expect, but on balance, being with the woman you love makes everything else worthwhile."

Matthew was counting on exactly that.

12

Laila had been out of sorts all day. Here it was, Christmas Eve. She was in Ireland. The man she loved was here, as well. She was surrounded by people she adored. And she had this mountain of packages that needed to be wrapped before morning. Usually it was a task she enjoyed.

And yet her mood was dark. She couldn't be sure if it was because Matthew had again refused to sleep with her the night before or if, as *he* suspected, she was miserable over the situation with her parents. She feared the latter was a bigger part of it than she cared to acknowledge.

She thought she'd successfully buried her hurt and disillusionment. How could she be missing two people who'd made it plain just how unimportant she was, or at least how little respect they had for her professional skills?

In her mind the two things were inseparable. She

was, in many ways, her work. It shouldn't be that way, but there it was. She'd been willing to pour her heart and soul into that community bank, just as her father had done. To have that kind of family loyalty and commitment rejected had wounded her deeply.

Why should she be the one to reach out to make amends? she wondered irritably while fighting with a piece of tape that had stuck to the wrapping paper in the wrong place. She ripped it loose and tossed the whole mess onto the floor, which was already littered with scraps of colorful paper she'd managed to ruin.

At this rate not one package would be ready for the celebration Mick had arranged for them in a private dining room first thing in the morning. She was sure he had his well-paid hotel elves hard at work in there already, putting up a tree and creating an atmosphere for the kids, who were expecting Santa to find them even across the ocean from Chesapeake Shores.

She had to admit she was looking forward to the chaos herself, and to seeing the expressions of delight on Carrie and Caitlyn's faces, as well as those of Davy, Henry and little Mick. Bree and Jake's baby and Kevin and Shanna's newborn were still too young to fully appreciate Mick's effort.

And she couldn't help wondering, with a flutter of anticipation in her stomach, if that would be the moment Matthew would choose for his proposal. Surely he wouldn't do it in front of the entire family and risk the embarrassment of a rejection.

Not that there was much risk. He'd made certain of that, reeling her in with the cleverness of a fisherman who knew just how much line to let out before setting the hook solidly.

"Oh, drat," she muttered as more tape twisted around and stuck to her and itself, rather than the package. "I should have bought gift bags and stuffed everything in those."

A knock on her door had her jumping up gratefully. Any interruption was welcome at this point. She found Jess and Connie on her doorstep.

"Why are you shut away in your room?" Jess demanded, brushing past her, then glancing at the mess. "Ah-ha. Why didn't you buy gift bags?"

"I was just wondering the same thing," Laila admitted, then glanced at Connie. "You look a little green. Are you okay?"

Connie nodded, then swallowed hard and darted past her to the bathroom.

"We think it's morning sickness," Jess confided. "She's been like this for the past couple of hours."

Laila grinned as understanding dawned. "She's pregnant? Already? Good grief, didn't she just decide a couple of days ago that she might want to be?"

"We don't know for sure, but apparently fate had already made its decision," Jess responded. "I keep trying to convince her to go for a home test, but I think she's in a state of shock."

"Thomas is going to be over the moon," Laila said. "Can you imagine his expression on Christmas morning if she tells him then? She couldn't give him a better gift."

"It'll be a lot better than the antiquarian book on the Chesapeake she lugged along to give him," Jess agreed.

"Could you keep her occupied while I run out and pick up the test? If I hand it to her, she won't be able to resist taking it."

"Go," Laila said. "I'll put her to work wrapping presents. I seem to be all thumbs."

Jess hesitated. "Is there a story behind that?"

"Maybe," Laila said.

"Then I'll hurry," Jess promised. "Don't reveal a thing till I'm back."

"If then," Laila murmured, shutting the door behind her.

When Connie finally emerged from the bathroom, she gave Laila an apologetic look. "Sorry about the grand entrance. I haven't been feeling well."

"Are you sure what you're feeling isn't pregnant?" Laila asked gently. "You did say you and Thomas hadn't done anything to avoid getting pregnant."

Connie shook her head. "I can't be. It's happened too fast. At my age people have to work at getting pregnant. We've been married only a few months."

"When those little swimmers are potent, it only takes one time," Laila teased her. "Surely you're not so ancient that you don't recall the lectures from health class."

Connie merely moaned at Laila's weak attempt at humor.

"But I haven't prepared Jenny for the idea," she protested. "She's going to be horrified. She's been an only child for her entire nineteen years. To be honest, she's probably a little spoiled. My brother and I went overboard to make up for her father virtually abandoning her. She wasn't all that happy when her uncle Jake and

Bree had a baby, at least not until the first time she held her. Then she got a little weepy. How on earth will she feel when I bring home a new baby?"

"Okay, she's used to being spoiled, but come on, Connie, she's away at college," Laila said, trying to reason with her. "She's building her own life. Surely she can't expect you to dote on her forever."

"I think she was expecting the next people I'd spoil would be her children, not another of my own," Connie said wryly.

"Let's say she's shocked at first," Laila conceded. "She'll come around, especially once the baby is born, just as she did with Bree and Jake's baby. She'll finally be a big sister. I'm sure that's something she pleaded to be for years."

"It was, until she realized that not only would it require that I have a man in my life, but it would dilute the attention I could pay to her." Connie shook her head, her expression filled with worry. "I honestly don't think she's going to take it well, and I don't want her attitude to spoil this for Thomas. If it's true, I don't want to know about it till after we're back home and Jenny's away at school. That'll give Thomas and me time to actually adapt to the news, and I'll be able to work out the best way to tell Jenny."

"I hear what you're saying, but you're going to have to fend off Jess," Laila warned. "She's out right this minute buying a home pregnancy test. She's romanticized the whole idea of you telling Thomas on Christmas morning." Laila gave Connie a rueful look. "Okay, we both have."

Despite her openly declared fears, Connie's expression turned dreamy. "It would be an amazing gift, wouldn't it?"

Thinking of how ecstatic Trace was, Laila could only nod. "Do you want to deny him—and yourself—that moment because of how Jenny might react? You could keep it just between the two of you for now. Jenny and everyone else could stay in the dark until you're back home."

Connie laughed. "Can you honestly see Thomas keeping such a secret without being locked in our room with the phone disconnected?"

Laila laughed with her. "You have a point."

Just then Jess returned, her expression triumphant as she tossed a pharmacy bag to Connie. "Do it now," she ordered.

Connie shook her head. "I can't."

Laila took Connie's ice-cold hand between hers. "Sweetie, I really did hear everything you said, but I agree with Jess. You need to do the test. You could be fretting over nothing. It's better to know. Then you can decide how you want to handle the news."

"Oh, believe me, I know already," Connie said. "I haven't felt like this since I was carrying Jenny." She held up the kit. "This will only confirm it."

Jess sat on her other side and held her other hand. "We'll be right here with you. If you decide to wait to tell Thomas and everyone else, that's up to you, but it'll give you peace of mind to know for sure."

Connie stared at Jess incredulously. "Peace of mind? In what universe does the prospect of a baby at my age bring about peace of mind? It'll mean years of diapers and toilet training and pre-school and science projects and teenage angst." Her eyes grew wider with each word. "Oh, my God, what were we thinking?"

Jess gave her a reassuring look. "You were thinking that you love Thomas and that this is your chance to have a child with a man who will be right there with you every single step of the way. You know he will be, Connie," she said earnestly. "It won't be the way it was with Sam. Thomas is going to be an amazing father. You're going to raise an incredible little O'Brien."

"As if the world needs another one," Laila muttered.

Both women turned to stare at her. "Are O'Briens the enemy again today?" Jess asked, amused.

"I believe so," Laila admitted. "One of them is particularly annoying."

"And yet weren't you and Matthew quite cozy at Dillon's last night?" Connie teased. "And didn't I see the two of you crawling into the back of a taxi together after the party?"

Laila scowled at her. "Yes, and your point would be…?"

"Just wondering what happened between there and here to put you in this mood," Connie said. "And before you even think of trying to deny that you're in a mood, the mess in this room suggests you've been taking your frustration out on the wrapping paper."

Jess grinned. "The mess in this room testifies to her *frustration.* What's really wrong, Laila? Wouldn't Matthew sleep with you last night?"

"He wants to wait until our wedding night," Laila blurted before she could censor herself. "Can you believe that? As if sex is some carrot-and-stick that will get me to walk down the aisle."

"And is it?" Jess inquired. "My cousin definitely seems capable of putting a glow on your cheeks."

"Whatever glow I've had on my cheeks was probably because he'd ticked me off," Laila retorted.

Connie held up her hands. "Is this really about sex, ladies? Isn't it actually about Laila's panic that Matthew is going to propose any second? That has my vote."

"Now that you mention it, I'll go along with that," Jess said readily.

Both women looked to Laila. She sighed. "I really despise the fact that the two of you know me so well. Yes, I hate knowing that it's coming, but I have no idea when or under what conditions. I don't know for sure if he's going to push for a wedding before we leave Ireland. Or whether I should say no, if he does, and insist on waiting. Everything's moving too fast."

"And you feel as if it's out of your control," Jess guessed.

Laila nodded. "Way, way out of my control."

"Have you lost your ability to say no?" Connie asked, trying unsuccessfully to hide a grin.

"Of course not," Laila replied. At least she'd never had any difficulty before. There were a dozen committees around town that could attest to that.

"Then it's not out of your control, is it?" Connie said reasonably. "I think all Matthew's really hoping is that you'll say yes. Beyond that, I imagine most of the details are negotiable."

Jess gave her a thoughtful look. "Unless the real problem is that you're warming to the idea of an impulsive trip down the aisle. Are you? Getting married right here would be pretty awesome."

Laila hadn't even wanted to admit it to herself, but she was. Once she'd gotten over her initial annoyance at all the planning and scheming that had gone on behind her back, she'd realized there was something romantic and unpredictable about it. It suited this new persona she'd been creating with Matthew. And it would probably horrify her parents, an added benefit these days.

"I suppose I am," she admitted to them. "Does that make me insane?"

"Not in my book," Jess said.

"Or mine," Connie agreed.

Jess studied her closely. "Does that mean you'll say yes?"

Laila drew in a deep breath, then slowly let it out. "It means I'll say yes." Then she frowned at her friends. "But you are not to tell Matthew that. You're not even to mention that the subject of a proposal, a wedding or anything like that came up. Are we clear about that? It would be totally weird for you two to be leaking information about my state of mind to him."

"My lips are sealed," Connie said at once. "Because I expect the same in return when it comes to this possible—*probable*—pregnancy of mine."

Jess looked disappointed, but she nodded. "Agreed on both points," she said reluctantly. She gave Connie a hopeful look. "Couldn't you at least take the test so we know for sure?"

Connie glanced at the package she'd carefully set away from her on the bed. "I suppose it couldn't hurt to know," she said, though without much enthusiasm.

A few minutes later, she emerged from the bathroom, a dazed expression on her face. "I'm pregnant," she said as if she hadn't been anticipating the result, despite her earlier claims. "I'm really pregnant."

Laila rushed to hug her, then realized Connie was actually a little weak-kneed. She eased her down onto the edge of the bed, then held her hands tightly.

"It's going to be okay," Laila reassured her. "Just like Jess said, this is going to be one amazing, lucky baby to have you and Thomas for parents."

"A baby," Connie repeated, her eyes suddenly filling with tears. "Thomas and I are having a baby." She gave them a wobbly smile. "Isn't that incredible?"

"Incredible," Laila confirmed.

"The best news ever," Jess agreed.

Connie stood and headed for the door. "I need to see Thomas."

As soon as the door closed behind her, Jess and Laila exchanged an amused look and started laughing.

"So much for keeping the news secret," Jess said.

"Did you think for one second she could keep it to herself?" Laila asked.

"No, which is exactly why I wanted her to take that test. I knew the results would send her running straight to Thomas," Jess replied, looking very pleased with herself.

Laila shook her head. "You're definitely an O'Brien."

"Well, of course I am," Jess said. "And darn proud of it." She paused then grinned. "Well, at least most of the time."

Nell slipped away from the hotel the day after Dillon's party and walked to the tobacco shop, hoping to find Dillon there. They'd had no time alone the night before. She'd considered it the better part of discretion to leave with Mick and the rest of the family. Only Luke had stayed behind, obviously hoping to score a few points with the intractable Moira. Nell was dying to know how that had turned out.

She found the shop jammed with last-minute Christmas shoppers in search of pipes, tobacco and Cuban cigars for holiday gifts. Despite the frenzy, Dillon's expression brightened when he caught sight of her.

"Go on into the office and start a pot of water for tea," he suggested. "I'll be with you as soon as I can be."

"Are you sure this is a good time? I didn't expect to find the place so busy, though of course I should have known it would be a bit of a madhouse on Christmas Eve."

"I've put my grandsons to work, along with my other employees. They'll be glad not to have me looking over their shoulders," he insisted. "Give me five minutes, perhaps ten."

"Take as long as you need."

She went into the once-familiar office, put the water on to boil, then took a seat. She realized she felt as comfortable in the small room now as she had as a teenage girl. Though it was a different leather chair after all these years, it felt much the same as she settled into it with her cup of tea and a book of poetry she'd found on the corner of Dillon's desk. The rich scent of tobacco drifted on the air all around her.

She closed her eyes and memories came flooding back, of sneaking kisses with Dillon in this very room, of her grandfather's benevolent smile even as he scolded them about their mischief, of the day she'd asked Dillon to walk with her and told him of her plan to leave Ireland forever and marry another man, a man of her parents' choosing, when she got back home. Even though her grandparents had told her to follow her heart, she'd been unable to ignore the wishes of the two people back home who meant the world to her.

And she'd known she would have a good life with Charles O'Brien. That much, at least, had turned out exactly as she'd envisioned it.

Still, on that awful day of what would be her last summer in Dublin, she'd been so sure she'd never recover from the heartbreak she'd seen in Dillon's eyes, but she had bounced back. In fact, she'd gone on to live a happy, full life in the area along the bay that had eventually become Chesapeake Shores.

"Sneaking a nap?" Dillon inquired.

His softly spoken words immediately brought her upright.

"Just remembering things," she corrected. "I have so many memories of this shop, this room." She met his gaze. "You."

"Good ones, I hope."

"Most of them, yes," she said. "Except for the day I told you I was leaving."

"That was a difficult day for both of us, I think. It was as hard on you in some ways as it was on me, hearing the news."

She nodded, relieved that he understood that it hadn't been an easy decision to make. "I don't regret the life I had, but I regret hurting you. I always felt I'd led you on, made promises I knew I couldn't keep."

"Water long since under the bridge," Dillon said.

"We've had a chance to reconnect now, Nell. I'll always be grateful for that."

"Me, as well," she told him, surprising tears filling her eyes.

He stepped closer, bent down and wiped the tears from her cheeks. "What's this about?"

She laughed. "I'm not entirely sure. It seems I'm feeling a bit sentimental today." She shook off the nostalgia. "How did things go after I left last night? Were Luke and Moira still speaking?"

"Loudly," he said with amusement. "I haven't heard that much arguing with such passion behind it in a very long time. I have to admit I'm completely baffled by the way they've taken to each other. Moira's being impossible, as always. Luke seems completely enchanted by it. What sort of courting is that?"

"The best kind, in some ways," Nell said. "Fireworks are an essential ingredient in the best marriages. They're especially important to the young, I think."

"Not at our age," Dillon said. "I'm not sure I have the will left or the strength for that kind of commotion."

She smiled at him. "Ah, but we've had years to discover that other things are far more important in the end—friendship, companionship, understanding."

"And respect," Dillon added.

"Absolutely."

He searched her face. "I think we have those things, Nell. Do you?"

"I believe we do."

He nodded, seemingly satisfied.

There were so many things she wanted to ask, so many decisions she felt needed to be made, but for now she settled for only one. "Will we see you at our Christmas celebration tomorrow?" she asked. "Mick's promised it will be something from a storybook for the benefit of the children."

"Then we can hardly miss it, can we?" Dillon responded. "I believe Kiera's actually looking forward to it. She seems quite taken with your family dynamics." He smiled. "You won her over, Nell. I'm grateful for that. And I'm relieved that Mick is the one who asked us to join you. Perhaps he, too, is mellowing."

Nell chuckled at his optimism. "Oh, I think he's just trying to keep us in plain sight so he knows what we're up to."

Dillon laughed. "Either way, I'm looking forward to it."

"So am I. Now I need to leave you to handle that horde of shoppers in the other room. I know you're worried that your grandsons will manage to send even these highly motivated shoppers off without making a sale."

"More worried that they'll simply give away the store," he said. "They've been infected by the holiday spirit, or perhaps a bit too much Guinness."

He walked with her to the door. "Shall I get a taxi for you?"

"No need. I'll walk back. It's another gorgeous day. I know enough not to take the sun here for granted."

He bent down and kissed her cheek. "Then I'll see you tomorrow. I'll save my Christmas wishes for then."

Down the block, she glanced back and saw him still standing in the doorway, staring after her much as he had on that day so long ago. This time, though, there was a smile on his lips and a jauntiness to his wave.

She couldn't help being glad that no matter what happened between them, she'd created happier memories for both of them this time.

Though the entire family was gathering for a private Christmas Eve dinner later, Matthew didn't think he could wait that long to hear the sound of Laila's voice. The day had been excruciatingly long without any sight of her. He called her room.

"I've some gifts here in need of wrapping," he said. "Would you care to volunteer?"

She laughed. "You must be kidding. I made such a mess of mine that I had to go out and spend a fortune on gift bags. Until I started counting, I hadn't realized just how overboard I'd gone on presents."

"Is there one for me?" he teased.

"More than one, if you must know, but that's all I'm telling you. Now, if you want to buy gift bags, I can tell you where to go, and you'd best be hurrying. I believe the stores have early closing hours today."

"You could come with me," he said hopefully. "It'll be much easier to show me than to tell me, don't you think?"

She hesitated, then said, "I can do that."

"Then I'll be by your room to pick you up in five minutes. Can you be ready?"

"Of course I can. You know I'm not a dawdler."

When he knocked on her door, she was bundled up as if they were heading to the North Pole.

"Has the weather taken an unexpected turn for the worse?" he asked, amused. "Last time I looked, the sun was shining and the temperature was above freezing."

"I bought the cashmere scarf, hat and gloves for myself today, and I couldn't wait to wear them," she said. "Feel how soft they are."

He took her hand in his. He preferred her bare skin, but the gloves were, indeed, soft, and the color of pink cotton candy. The scarf and hat, thankfully, were a muted plaid with just a hint of that same pink, enough to bring out the color in her cheeks.

"Lovely," he murmured, his gaze on her face and not the cashmere accessories.

She blinked at the intensity of his gaze, and the color in her cheeks deepened. "We need to hurry," she said, urging him along to the elevator.

Inside, he pulled her to him, then settled his mouth over hers for a deep, lingering kiss.

"Hot," she whispered brokenly, tugging at the scarf when he'd released her.

"Just wanted you to see that there are far better ways to stay warm," he taunted, as they emerged onto the street. "Now, which way?"

She regarded him blankly. "Which way?"

"To buy the gift bags," he reminded her, grinning.

She glanced around, got her bearings eventually, then headed off. When he didn't immediately follow, she turned and scowled at him. "What now?"

"Just admiring the view," he said.

"Has anyone mentioned today how impossible you are?"

He shook his head. "It didn't come up while I was shopping," he said, as if he were considering the question carefully. "And I spoke to a few different people in the family. No, not that I recall. 'Impossible' wasn't mentioned once."

"Well, it should have been," she said with feigned exasperation. "I can't be the only one who sees it."

"Oh, wait, there was one slightly testy exchange with your brother," he admitted. "It might have been implied in that."

Her expression immediately turned wary. "You spoke to Trace?"

"I did."

"About what?"

"This and that," he said.

"Matthew, do not be evasive. What did you discuss with my brother?"

"I don't have to tell you everything."

"You do if you expect our relationship to last more than another minute or two," she countered.

He studied her. "So, secrets are a deal breaker?"

"Definitely."

He nodded. "Good to know."

"Well?"

"Well what?"

"You and Trace," she said impatiently. "What happened?"

"We talked. We agreed on a few things eventually." He shrugged. "That was about it."

"You are being deliberately evasive, and I want to go on record that I don't like it." She shrugged. "Never mind. I'll just get the truth out of Trace."

Matthew laughed. "I doubt that."

"Oh, I have my ways," she said direly.

"Those ways of yours might work on me," he admitted, grinning. "I doubt they're effective on your brother."

"I have *different* ways of dealing with him," she said.

He shook his head. "I wouldn't count on those working, either. Guys have a code of honor, you know. It pretty much implies pain of death and all that."

"You're not taking me seriously," she grumbled.

"Your threats, not so much," he agreed, then looked into her eyes. "You, however, I take very, very seriously."

And tonight he intended to prove to her just how serious his intentions were.

13

Christmas Eve dinner, despite being in a hotel dining room, was a festive occasion. With Mick's encouragement and generous tipping and, Laila suspected, some advice from Nell, the staff had gone out of its way to create a cozy and warm holiday atmosphere, to say nothing of a traditional feast. There was to be roasted goose, spiced beef, Yorkshire pudding, a potato-apple stuffing and, she'd heard, an Irish Mist trifle for dessert.

Laila stood just inside the door and took in the long table with its white tablecloth, beautiful china and silverware, the candles in a row down the center, far from the reach of small hands. Bowls of holly and greens gave the table color, along with the traditional Christmas crackers that would be popped to reveal a variety of treats.

The children, far too excited to sit still, were racing around the room with only the occasional admonition from an adult to settle down.

The adults were clustered in small groups, glasses of wine in hand, chattering as if they hadn't seen each other in months, rather than hours. One of the best things about this family, in Laila's opinion, was how much they truly seemed to enjoy each other's company. It was so different from the stiff, formal occasions she'd grown used to at home.

Eventually she spotted Matthew across the room, deep in conversation with Mick. She frowned at their too-serious expressions, wondering if Matthew was conspiring with his uncle after all to keep Nell and Dillon apart.

Only one way to find out for sure, she thought, crossing the room to join them. She considered it her duty to stand up for Nell if no one else was around to do it, though why she felt it necessary was difficult to explain. Surely there were at least some O'Briens on Nell's side. Megan and Susie came immediately to mind, but they were nowhere to be found at the moment.

"So, you really have no objections to assigning Jaime to take over the project in Florida," Matthew said, referring to Mick's second-in-command, Jaime Alvarez, who'd been all but running the company the past few years. "You don't think it will cause problems?"

Mick regarded him affectionately. "Not under the circumstances, no. Jaime's credentials are solid, and he likes to be on-site from time to time. He'll be happy to take over. You'll still lead the design team and give the developer the fresh, innovative architecture they're looking for. You'll make the occasional site visit, as necessary. It's all good, Matthew."

Matthew regarded him with relief. "Thanks, Uncle Mick."

Mick gave Laila a conspiratorial wink that she couldn't begin to understand. Obviously this had nothing to do with Nell and Dillon.

"All for a good cause," Mick said, then left them alone.

Laila studied Matthew curiously. "What was that about?"

"Just rearranging a few things at work," he said.

"Were you talking about the Florida project?" she asked. "Mick didn't take you off it, did he?" Her indignation mounted at the thought of Mick treating Matthew so shabbily after dangling the development of an entire seaside community in front of him.

"Actually I asked to be taken off the on-site supervision," Matthew said.

She tried to wrap her mind around that and couldn't. "But, Matthew, this was your big break," she protested. "Why would you do that?"

"I have more important things on my schedule at the moment," he said, holding her gaze. "And since you were standing right here, I know you heard Uncle Mick. I'll still design the whole project."

"But to manage it start to finish," she said. "Weren't you really looking forward to the chance to watch your ideas come to fruition?"

"There will be other projects, Laila," he said, clearly unfazed by the turn of events. "I'm comfortable with my decision or I wouldn't have made it and gone to Mick for his approval."

"I just don't understand," she said. A few days ago

he'd been so thrilled by this opportunity. Why would he give it up?

Suddenly she recalled their conversation several days before and his mention that the timing for this was all wrong, given the status of their relationship.

She looked into Matthew's eyes. "Please tell me you didn't give this up because of us," she said. "Matthew, I don't want to be responsible for you losing out on a chance to make your mark in your career."

"You're not responsible," he insisted. "Stop worrying, Laila. Didn't I just say I made the decision all on my own?"

She still wasn't satisfied. "Did I play any role at all in that decision?"

"Of course I took you into consideration, just as I always will," he said.

Though he seemed perfectly happy with what he'd done, she couldn't help comparing it to her own situation. "You didn't have to give up something in your career just because I threw mine away," she told him.

He had the audacity to laugh at that. "Is that what you think? That I was trying to level the career playing field in some twisted way?"

"Weren't you?"

"Absolutely not." He gave her hand a squeeze. "I swear to you this is all good, Laila. Right now, you'll just have to take my word on that."

She wanted to, but she spent most of dinner fretting over the conversation she'd overheard and what Matthew had said in response to her questions. She was sure it must be killing him to give up control of such a huge project. This was the kind of thing that could make his reputation, just as Chesapeake Shores had made Mick's. Why would he make such a sacrifice when it wasn't necessary, at least not from her point of view?

Midway through the meal, Mick stood up and raised his glass. "I won't make one of my long-winded speeches tonight," he assured them to much laughter and applause. "I just want to thank all of you for making this trip to Ireland something we'll all remember for years to come. Each one of you has an important role in this family, and it wouldn't have been the same if any one of you hadn't been able to be with us, right, Ma?"

Nell nodded, her cheeks damp with tears. "I'm so grateful, especially to you, Susie, for ensuring that this trip happened. Coming back to Dublin once more has meant the world to me."

Susie leaned over and hugged her grandmother. "It was my pleasure, Gram." She winked at Mack. "It hasn't been a bad honeymoon, either."

"Indeed, it hasn't," Mack said, his gaze on his wife filled with adoration.

Mick cleared his throat. "As *I* was saying…"

Nell gave him an impudent look. "Sorry to steal your moment in the spotlight," she said, without much remorse in her tone.

"Thank you all for being here," Mick continued. "There's an Irish blessing my father often said on Christmas Eve. It sums up what I wish for each of you. 'The light of the Christmas star to you. The warmth of home and hearth to you. The cheer and goodwill of friends to you. The hope of a childlike heart to you. The joy of a thousand angels to you. The love of the Son and God's peace to you.'"

His eyes seemed a little misty as he added, "My thanks to each of you for making this family something so special. Merry Christmas to all!"

"Is it time for Santa yet?" Davy called out hopefully.

Mick chuckled. "Not just yet. Don't you worry, though. He knows where to find you. And I guarantee this is going to be a holiday to remember."

Laila turned to look at Matthew beside her and caught his gaze on her. "You look a bit like the cat that swallowed the canary," she said, studying him. "What's that about?"

"Just thinking about what Uncle Mick said," he told her.

"About it being a memorable holiday?"

He nodded.

She smiled. "I can't argue with that. It already is. Ireland has been everything I expected and then some."

"And it's only going to get better," he said mysteriously.

The look in his eyes made her heart skip a beat. Was he planning what she thought he might be? Was he finally going to propose? Since she wasn't about to ask such a thing, she merely lifted a brow. "You have some pull with Santa?"

"You bet. I've had him on standby for weeks."

"I'm surprised, then, that you didn't get him or his elves to wrap all those packages for you, instead of conning me into doing it with promises of hot chocolate."

"You're much prettier than Santa," he said seriously. "I'd always rather spend time with you." He stood up. "Why don't we get our coats and head over to the church? With a crowd the size of this one, someone will need to go ahead and save seats."

"We'll come with you," Jess said, dragging Will to his feet. "I need to walk off that meal anyway."

Laila was surprised and a little disappointed when Matthew didn't refuse Jess's offer. Clearly he hadn't intended to propose en route to the church, or else he was amazingly unfazed by a last-second change to his plan. Maybe, once the cat had gotten out of the bag, he'd decided against proposing to her here in Ireland. Maybe she'd been twisting herself into knots over a decision she wouldn't even have to make.

She should have felt relief, but as the hours till midnight ticked by, she couldn't help regretting that she might not get that romantic Christmas Eve proposal, after all.

On the ride to the church, Nell glanced over at her son and decided it was time to get things out in the open once and for all.

"Mick, as long as we have a few minutes, there are some things we need to discuss," she said. She glanced toward Megan and saw her give an encouraging nod.

Mick regarded her with dismay. "This is about Dillon, I assume."

"It is."

"And you want to spoil Christmas Eve by having this conversation now?"

"Earlier you seemed full of holiday cheer and goodwill. I'm hoping that will extend to this."

Megan gave him a warning look. "Listen to her,

Mick. For once, don't think of yourself or even the family. Listen to what your mother wants for herself."

He frowned at both of them. "Are the two of you in cahoots, then?"

"I haven't said a word to Megan," Nell assured him.

"Okay, fine," he grumbled. "Let's put all our cards on the table. I'm not happy about what I've seen going on."

Nell smiled. "And what is it you think you've seen? Two old friends getting reacquainted? Is there something wrong with that?"

"Of course not, but I've seen the looks between you," Mick said. "There's no denying that there's something more there."

"I hope so," Nell said. "But we've not discussed it, and we've certainly made no decisions. If and when that happens, I promise you'll be the first to know."

Mick gave her a resigned look. "Then you'll stay right here in Dublin if he asks?"

"I don't know what I'll do," Nell admitted. "But it's nice to know that at my age, I might have the option of finding happiness with someone. Someday you'll understand what a blessing that is. In fact, you should understand it now, since you've only recently had Megan come back into your life. Can you deny your days are richer because of it?"

"Of course not," Mick replied.

Megan chuckled and reached for his hand. "Good answer."

Mick only frowned. "Well, if Dillon hasn't asked anything and you haven't decided anything, then why are we even talking about this?" he asked irritably.

"Because I want you to fire that investigator you

hired," she said, holding his gaze until he looked chagrined. "Yes, I know all about that, and I find it insulting. You're behaving as if I haven't a brain in my head."

"Come on, Ma, it's my job to look after you."

She placed a hand on his arm. "Mick, I know you've
taken it as your duty ever since your father died to look
after me, just as you've looked after your children, but
I'm not one of them. I'm your mother, and I think we
can agree that I've done nothing over the years to make
you think I'm not strong, capable and smart."

"And wise," Megan added.

"Thank you," Nell said.

"I never denied any of that," Mick said. "You're all
of those things."

"But you're behaving as if none of it is true," Nell
said. "Fire the investigator, Mick. I insist on it. And tomorrow, when Dillon and his family join us, treat them
with more than courtesy."

Mick's frown deepened. "Meaning what? Have I
been anything less than polite to them since our first
meeting?"

"No, you've minded your manners very diligently,"
she admitted. "But I'd like to see you spend time with
them with an open heart. You might actually find that
you like them."

Mick looked skeptical. "Even that Moira girl?"

Nell laughed. "Even her. She could be a part of the
family a lot sooner than Dillon."

"That's Jeff's worry, not mine," Mick said with exaggerated relief. "If I were him, I'd have a serious talk
with Luke before things get out of hand."

"Well, fortunately for Luke, you're not his father,"

Nell said. "And I'll thank you to remember that and keep your opinion to yourself."

Mick sighed and gave her a rueful look. "You're taking all the fun out of this for me."

"And the worry, too, I hope," Nell said. "Things have a way of working out as they should without any help from you."

"Amen to that," Megan said. She gave her husband's hand a squeeze. "Perhaps you could spend all of this spare time you'll suddenly have focusing on me."

Mick gave her a lingering look that slowly brightened. "I imagine I could do that."

"There now," Nell said with satisfaction. "It's turning out to be a happy Christmas, just the way we all envisioned it to be."

Mick didn't look entirely convinced, but she had high hopes she'd made her point and that he'd leave her free to follow whatever path promised the greatest happiness.

Matthew knew that Laila was rattled by his failure to propose at some point during the day. He'd seen a hint of disappointment in her eyes earlier in the afternoon when they'd been alone in his room, putting gifts into bags for tomorrow's celebration. He'd seen it again tonight when Jess and Will had joined them for the walk to the church for Christmas Eve Mass. Exactly as he'd hoped, she seemed to be anticipating the proposal now, rather than dreading it.

And he was more than ready to go for broke, to stake his claim for the future he wanted with her. He'd cleared the last hurdle earlier when he'd talked to Mick about having Jaime take over the on-site management for the Florida project. He had the rest of the plan all worked out in his head, kept going over it even as the carols reverberated in the old church and the priest's words echoed. As he gazed around the candlelit interior, he couldn't help imagining Laila walking down the center aisle toward him. Lost in the images, he hoped God would forgive him for his lack of attentiveness just this once, and asked His blessing for what he had planned for later.

By the end of the service he should have been jittery with nerves, but he was suddenly calm and eager to take this next step in his relationship with Laila.

As they left the church amid wishes for a happy Christmas from complete strangers, Gram, his parents, Mick and Megan left for the hotel in the car Mick had arranged for them. The rest of them chose to walk back through the now-deserted streets, past darkened shops lit only by Christmas lights twinkling in the windows. Shanna had remained at the hotel with the smallest children, but Caitlyn, Carrie, Henry and Davy were practically bouncing with excitement, and chattering about everything they hoped Santa would leave for them.

Eventually Matthew fell into step beside Laila. A warning glance at Jess had her and Will quickly moving on, leaving the two of them to straggle along alone behind all the others. The sounds of the children's high-pitched voices faded.

Apparently aware of the look he'd cast at Jess and the increasing distance between themselves and the rest of the family, Laila regarded him with suspicion. "What's up with that scowl you gave Jess and Will, Matthew? No holiday spirit?"

"My holiday spirit is just fine," he said, considering it a bad sign that her mood had darkened and she'd already managed to put him on the defensive. "I thought maybe we could take a walk around the park. I'm not ready for bed just yet. How about you?"

She didn't seem impressed by the suggestion. "It's practically the middle of the night and you want to go for a stroll?"

"It's not as if we haven't walked around Chesapeake Shores at this hour," he reminded her. "Of course, on those occasions, you'd just scrambled out of my bed to make it safely home in the dark of night so no one would guess we were sleeping together."

She had the grace to wince at the reminder. "I know it seemed foolish and probably even demeaning to you, but I thought it was prudent. I've told you before that I'm sorry."

He realized this conversation was heading in the wrong direction fast. "No point in rehashing all of that," he said quickly. "What's done is done. It's time to move forward."

She studied him curiously. "What exactly are you proposing?"

Matthew fought a smile at her choice of words. He gestured toward a bench on the fringe of the park. "Sit here and I'll explain."

"Matthew, haven't you noticed that it's freezing out here? The temperature must have dropped twenty degrees since we left for church."

"If you'll just cooperate, this won't take that long," he retorted with exasperation.

"Cooperate how?" she asked testily.

Given how badly this seemed to be going, he wondered if he should reconsider, but he didn't want to give up just yet on the plan he'd envisioned.

"By not asking so many questions, for starters," he said with a touch of impatience. "For once can't you just take it on faith that what I have to say is important?"

It suddenly seemed to dawn on her what was going on. Eyes wide, she dutifully sat on the edge of the bench.

Matthew stood in front of her, his expression solemn as he prepared to get down on one knee. He'd hoped for a little moonlight to set the scene, but clouds seemed to have filled the sky and blocked it.

And then the rain began to fall. Not just a light drizzle, but a deluge. He could talk fast or risk pneumonia for both of them. Apparently this proposal of his wasn't meant to go smoothly or to be half as romantic as he'd intended. That was either a challenge or an omen. He preferred to think of it as the former.

"Never mind," he said, grabbing her hand. "Let's make a dash for it before we're soaked through. We'll finish this at the hotel."

Though they both had long legs and a powerful motivation, there was no way to escape being soaked to the skin by the time they reached the lobby.

"Gee, that was fun," Laila said, laughing as they ran, dripping, past the horrified doorman and straight to the elevators.

When the elevator reached Laila's floor, Matthew

exited with her and went straight to her room, then held out his hand for the key card.

"Tonight, with both of us looking like drowned rats, you want to come in?" she said, regarding him incredulously.

"We haven't finished talking," he said stubbornly, determined not to let a downpour steal this opportunity from him.

"Don't you want to dry off first?"

"I'll do that in your room," he said. "This place has plenty of towels on hand. I'm sure you can spare one for me."

She frowned but didn't argue. "I get the shower first," she declared instead.

Since those were the first promising words out of her mouth in a while, he nodded. "It's only fair," he said agreeably.

Inside, she tossed him a towel, then gulped as he immediately began stripping off his wet clothes. He glanced up and saw her throat working. "Something bothering you?" he asked.

Her cheeks flushed. "It's not that I'm not appreciative of the show, but what do you think you're doing?"

"Drying off," he said simply. "You should be, too." He noticed then that she didn't seem to be looking away. In fact, her gaze seemed to be pretty intense. It was yet another positive sign, and after weeks of abstinence, he was ready to seize such signs whenever they appeared.

"Laila? Are you sure there's not something on your mind?" He could only pray it was the same thing that was on his. The whole proposal plan had been wiped out by the sudden urgency of his desire to get her into that king-size bed across the room. All of the reasons that had been holding them back suddenly seemed unimportant.

"This is a really bad idea," she murmured, mostly to herself.

"This?"

"You and I getting naked in the same room," she said, though there was no mistaking the desire darkening her eyes.

His lips curved. "Seems to me as if it's the best idea either of us has had in a long time," he contradicted. "Let me help you with those wet clothes."

She shook her head, even as her gaze locked with his and she stepped forward, almost within reach.

"I'm getting mixed signals here," he told her, even as he began to close the distance between them.

"Believe me, I know," she said, shedding her coat to pool at her feet.

He waited, breath held, to make sure he wasn't mistaking her intentions. Her blouse and skirt followed until she was standing before him in only a lacy bra and matching panties that left most of her amazing body in full view.

Hand shaking, he touched the tip of her breast, felt the nipple immediately harden. He closed his eyes as a powerful, familiar need ripped through him.

"If you don't want this, Laila, you need to say so now."

"You're the one who's been saying no repeatedly," she reminded him with a slight curve of her lips.

"I've reconsidered."

"I'm glad," she said softly.

Without so much as a second's hesitation, she closed the remaining distance between them, linked her fingers behind his neck and lifted her mouth to his. The kiss was long, greedy and hot, an unmistakable invitation.

Thank goodness.

He might have to put his proposal on hold till morning, if the night went the way he was anticipating, but this was the kind of delay he could get totally behind.

14

"Happy Christmas," Laila murmured into Matthew's ear just after dawn on Christmas morning.

"Happy doesn't begin to describe it," he said, smiling.

"Don't be smug. We've always known that this isn't the problem between us."

"There are no problems between us," he corrected. "Just way too much outside interference."

She chuckled. "I wonder if my parents would like being referred to as *outside interference*."

"It would probably make them nuts," Matthew conceded. "But they're not here right now. I say we should make the most of it."

Laila moaned softly. "I'm not sure I have the stamina left for that. Besides, we're probably expected downstairs. Given how excited the kids were last night, they probably haven't slept a wink. They're going to want to open presents soon."

"This is more important," Matthew told her. He sat up, plumped up the piles of down pillows, then pulled her up next to him. "Remember that talk I wanted to have last night?"

"The one that almost got us drowned?" she said, amusement threading through her voice. "I remember."

"I planned to have it here once we'd dried off, but then someone distracted me," he reminded her.

"You were the one who stripped off his clothes," she countered.

"Can't deny that," he agreed. "And here I go getting distracted again."

"I could probably keep your attention focused on me for quite a while," she teased.

"Stamina," he reminded her. "You said I'd worn you out. Believe me when I tell you that this is all about you. Now, will *you* please focus?"

She made an exaggerated show of glancing at her wrist, though her watch was on the bedside table. "Two minutes, pal. Talk fast. Something tells me little O'Brien people are going to be stirring any minute, and we'll have that command performance downstairs."

Matthew gave her an exasperated look. "Pour on the pressure, why don't you? Okay, here it is in the condensed, but no less heartfelt, version. Are you ready?"

Her pulse scrambled, and her heart thundered in her chest. Unable to speak around the sudden lump in her throat, she nodded. This was it. No more joking around. She looked into his eyes, saw the love shining there and knew without a doubt that this was the moment she'd been awaiting far longer than a few days.

He brushed a curl from her cheek, his gaze tender. "I

love you, Laila Riley. There's no news there. You're the most complicated, challenging, unpredictable woman I know, and I want to spend the rest of my life trying to unravel all of your mysteries. I refuse to do that in secret, so I'm asking you here and now to marry me, to tell the entire world how much we love each other."

She was about to speak when he touched a finger to her lips. "Hear me out," he insisted. "I want to get married right here, right now, before we leave Ireland, while we're surrounded by family. I can't imagine a better way to end this trip or a more important way to make the statement to the entire world that we're going home to start a new life together."

Laila couldn't seem to wrap her head around what he was saying. In essence she'd been expecting just this for days, but now that the proposal was on the table, the magnitude of what he was asking had left her speechless. She heard the words, understood what he wanted, but on some level it still made no sense to her.

Matthew did flings, not forever. Of course, she couldn't recall the last time there'd been even a hint that there was another woman in his life, not even while they'd been apart. He seemed to have been faithful for a long time now, even without a commitment from her. If she loved him—and she did—she had no reason not to trust his words, not to take the leap of faith into their future.

"You really do want to get married?" she asked, just to be sure. "Vows in front of a priest, the whole nine yards? You want to be with me forever?"

"Yes," he said solemnly, though there was the faintest hint that he was fighting a smile. "That can't come as a huge surprise. You must have been expecting this ever since the family let the cat out of the bag days ago."

"I know, I know, but I need to be sure this isn't just some in-your-face game you're playing to make my father even crazier. This is just about you and me, our future?"

"Believe me, your father has nothing to do with this. Did you miss the part when I said I love you?" He reached for his pants, then pulled a box out of the pocket. "Maybe this will convince you I'm serious."

He flipped open the box to reveal an impressive diamond engagement ring. Her eyes widened. "You're kidding me! Will I even be able to lift my hand?"

"Let's put it on and see," he suggested, clearly not taking offense.

When he reached for her hand, she snatched it away. She got out of bed, tugged the sheet off the bed, wrapped herself in it and began to pace, trying to work through her emotions. She thought she'd done that ages ago when she'd first heard about this crazy scheme for them to marry in Ireland, had even believed she'd been ready to plunge in without a single second thought. Why was she hesitating now?

Certainly her heart was shouting an emphatic yes. But the well-trained part of her that reacted calmly and rationally was telling her to take a step back, to go over that mental list of cons she always had in her head. The Laila Riley she'd always thought she was did not take a step of this magnitude without studying it from every angle. If there'd been a way to make spreadsheets for such things, she would have done it.

The Laila Riley she'd seen through Matthew's eyes,

however, took chances, trusted her heart. Just as Nell had encouraged her to do, she remembered, with the beginnings of a smile.

Matthew's gaze never once faltered. He actually seemed to understand the struggle she was waging with herself. Wasn't that one of the best things about him, that he truly understood her?

"Laila, do you love me?" he asked quietly, reducing things to the absolute basics.

"Yes," she responded without reservation.

This time he didn't even try to stop his smile. "Okay, then. Let's make it official. Let's be spontaneous and unpredictable."

She gave him a wry look. "It's hardly spontaneous and unpredictable with half your family making plans behind my back."

"Okay, I think there may be a few bridal gowns on hold, and Gram has spoken to the priest at the church we attended last night and looked into a special license. I think the path has been cleared. The real question is, do you want to marry me? And are you ready to do it now?"

Even though she'd known about this for days, it was all happening too fast. She swallowed hard. "How soon?"

"Tomorrow," he suggested. "The next day."

"Matthew, not even your extraordinary family can pull together a wedding that quickly," she protested.

"They think they can. I see no reason to start doubting them now. And if you want your folks to be here, you can call and invite them. Or Trace will speak to them. He's promised to do whatever it takes to get them over here. I'll even do the formal thing and request your father's permission to marry you, if you'd like me to."

She was surprised by his willingness to reach out. "You'd do that after the way he's behaved toward us?"

He held her gaze. "If it will make you happy, maybe help to mend fences, there's nothing I won't do." He studied her solemnly. "What's really holding you back? Did you want the big hoopla at home? If that's been your dream, then we'll go that route. Whatever you want."

"It's not that," she assured him. "Getting married here would be the most romantic thing I can imagine. And I loved that church last night. Any wedding there would be like something out of a storybook."

"Then what's holding you back?"

Before she could respond to that, her cell phone rang. She glanced at the caller ID and saw that it was the very man who'd been such a thorn in their sides.

"It's my father," she told Matthew, reaching for the phone. She drew in a deep breath and braced herself to take the call. "Dad? Merry Christmas!"

"It's not much of a Christmas with you and Trace all the way across the ocean," he grumbled.

Laila didn't respond. She wasn't going to start an argument, but she was prepared for one. The ball was in her father's court.

"You there, Laila?"

"I'm here."

"I've had a lot of time to think lately," he began. "And to listen to your mother and your brother, who've had plenty to say about my hardheadedness."

"I see."

"I think perhaps I was a little hasty in letting you

quit your job without fighting to change your mind. You were doing a good job at the bank."

Laila felt the tightness in her chest ease at the admission. "I appreciate that, Dad."

"Well, since you've come to your senses and ended that unfortunate business with Matthew, I'd like you to come back to work as soon as you get home. We'll find a way to get past all this nonsense and reassure people you're a sensible woman."

She should have been elated by the offer. But the string attached was huge enough to choke her. He assumed she was through with Matthew, when the opposite was true. And if that made her less than sensible in his view, well, so be it.

"Dad, who gave you the idea that Matthew and I are through?"

"Your brother assured me before you left for Ireland that was the case."

"Well, he was wrong," she said softly. "So if that's one of the conditions, then the answer has to be no."

She heard him suck in his breath. "Girl, have you lost your mind?" he demanded. "I can't have the entire town laughing at you behind your back for getting involved with a man who'll only wind up leaving you for another woman in a few weeks or a few months. It's what Matthew does. To say nothing of the fact that it makes you look like one of those jaguars or cougars, or whatever they call older women who go after younger men."

Laila could hear her mother in the background trying to no avail to calm him down. Laila knew then that it was all pointless. There was no going back.

"Actually, Dad, I have come to my senses," she told

him. "I'm in love with Matthew, and that's more important than any job."

"Nonsense!"

She sighed. "Tell me something, Dad, why did you really want me back?"

"Because this bank should stay under family control," he said adamantly. "And it's clear that your brother wants no part of it."

"Which leaves me," she said wearily, wondering why she was surprised that she was still second choice. Even if cutting Matthew out of her life weren't a deal breaker, she could never go back knowing that nothing had really changed.

Laila turned and looked at the man next to her on the bed, the very naked man whom she loved with all her heart. Given a choice between Matthew and the bank, between Matthew and her father's approval, there really was no choice at all. She'd gotten it right the night she'd quit her job, after all. Whatever resentment she'd felt since that night faded away.

She looked into Matthew's eyes. "Yes," she said softly, oblivious to the fact that she was still holding the phone.

"Did you just say yes?" her father bellowed as if he didn't trust the international phone signal.

She blinked and focused on the call that had changed everything. "I didn't say yes to you, Dad. I don't want your job, not with those particular strings attached. I was saying yes to Matthew's proposal of marriage."

"You're with him now?" her father demanded, his voice filled with indignation. "It's barely dawn over there. This is exactly what I was talking about, you making a spectacle of yourself with that man."

She managed a slow smile for the man beside her. "Sorry if that's your view of things, Dad. So you can't say I didn't tell you, just as soon as we can get a special license, we're going to be married." As she spoke, she never looked away from Matthew. "If you and Mother would like to be here for the wedding, book a flight and come on over. Despite all our differences, it would mean a lot to me to have you here."

"You're actually going to marry that man in Ireland?" her father asked incredulously.

She smiled at Matthew. "Yes, I am. Let me know if you're coming over."

At the mention of a wedding, she heard her mother trying to wrest the phone from her father, demanding to speak to her, but her father held tight.

"I'm calling your brother this minute," he warned. "He'll put an end to this insanity right now."

"I don't think so," she said as Matthew kissed her shoulder, then moved on until she could hardly catch her breath. "Gotta go. 'Bye, Dad. Merry Christmas to you and Mom."

She disconnected the call, tossed the phone aside and moved into Matthew's arms. It was certainly starting out to be the merriest holiday season she'd ever had. And something told her the best was yet to come.

Nell looked around the room Mick had had decorated for their family holiday celebration. There was a huge tree with a mountain of gifts under it. Her great-grandchildren were already tearing off wrapping paper and scattering gift bags in every direction. It was going to cost someone a fortune to get all of these things back to Chesapeake Shores. Still, whatever the cost, it was a small price to pay to see the delight in their eyes.

Next to her Kiera had an expression of astonishment on her face that was only in part due to the gift certificate Nell had given her for a full day of pampering at a Dublin spa.

"I've never been to a celebration quite like this," Kiera admitted. "It's like something from a storybook. The stores of Dublin should all be sending you notes of thanks."

"My family has a tendency to go overboard," Nell confessed. "I think it would bother me more if they weren't so generous to others, as well. Over the years we've made sure that even the littlest ones take presents to the homeless or Toys for Tots. They understand that we're blessed and meant to share."

"Perhaps some of that will rub off on my family," Kiera said, nodding toward her sons. "They've developed an unattractive sense of entitlement."

"Moira, as well?" Nell asked, looking at the young woman, who was feigning complete disinterest as Luke tried his best to charm her.

"Actually I've seen a change in her just in the past few days," Kiera confided. "I think she's finding it more and more difficult to remain immune to your grandson's charm. He's been a good influence on her." She met Nell's gaze. "Is he just playing a game, do you think?"

"All love affairs seem to start with a bit of a game," Nell said. "They only turn serious as time goes on. I do know Luke is an honorable man. He will never intentionally hurt her."

Kiera nodded. "That's good then."

Just then Dillon came back with cups of tea for them, a smile on his face. "I just had a perfectly civilized conversation with Mick," he told them, a hint of triumph in his voice. He held Nell's gaze. "I assume I have you to thank for that."

"Mick and I understand each other," Nell assured him. "Being Mick, I can't promise it will last, but he has vowed to try."

Kiera seemed to sense that the conversation was turning personal. She excused herself to give them privacy.

After she'd gone, Dillon said, "I like that Mick cares so deeply about what happens to you, Nell. It says a lot about the way you raised him. Jeff and Thomas, as well."

"And despite whatever issues there once were between you and your daughter, I see how much she cares about you," Nell said. She met his gaze. "Families belong together."

He looked deep into her eyes as if searching for the hidden meaning behind her words. "Does that mean you intend to return to Chesapeake Shores with yours?" he asked eventually, his expression sad.

Nell knew what he was asking. And the truth was that she'd missed many things about Dublin, the sights, the stores, the noisy, friendly pubs, the sound of an Irish lilt like the one in Dillon's voice. In the end, though, she preferred the peace of Chesapeake Shores. It was home.

She tried to picture Dillon there, in her cottage,

walking with her along the shore. It fit. It really did. She wondered if he would visit, maybe even stay.

Ignoring his question, she responded with one of her own. "Dillon, have you ever thought of coming to the States?"

He shook his head, his expression increasingly filled with sorrow as her intentions became more clear.

"I guess I've always thought of it as the place that took you away from me," he told her. "Of course, it was Charles O'Brien who did that, but it was hard to lay blame on him, when it was him you chose."

"I'm sorry I hurt you."

"It wasn't meant to be between the two of us back then," he said, sounding resigned. "Or now, I'm guessing. You were a bit too careful to avoid my question about going home."

She sighed at his ability to see through her. "To be honest, I just don't know what to do, Dillon. You were right before. My family means everything to me. I'm comfortable in my little cottage by the sea, surrounded by people I love." She held his gaze. "Would you at least consider coming for a visit now and then? I'd like to show you my world, have you be a part of it for however long you could stay."

"And I've been hoping I could entice you into staying on here, at least for a while," he said.

"But my family—" she protested, just as he'd obviously anticipated. But then she stopped herself.

Her sons and grandchildren were mostly grown, settled. They could spare her for a few more days, even a few more weeks. Didn't she owe it to herself and to Dillon to see what might come of this? Was it foolish

at her age to think they might find something meaningful together? It would be foolish only if she were
to throw caution to the wind and uproot herself on a
whim, she decided.

"I'll think about staying a bit longer, if you'll consider coming to Chesapeake Shores after that." She held
his gaze. "We're both comfortably off, Dillon. There's
no reason we couldn't spend time in both places, is
there?"

"A compromise?" he teased with exaggerated shock.
"The Nell I knew never compromised."

"I've learned a few things over the years. Life is
filled with compromises."

"It is," he agreed. "And if we're wise, we make them
happily and don't look back."

He lifted his hand, rested it gently against her cheek.
"I'm so glad we've had this chance to look back for just
a little while."

"Better, though," she told him, "is that we've given
each other hope in looking forward."

He smiled. "That it is, Nell. That it is."

Laila was about to take a sip of champagne amid the
chaos of Christmas morning with the O'Briens, when
Jess and Connie caught up with her and steered her
away from everyone else.

"What is the meaning of this?" Jess demanded, holding Laila's hand up to the light so that the diamond ring
sparkled brightly.

Laila grinned. "You're a smart woman. I'm sure you
can figure it out."

"You and Matthew are engaged!" Connie exclaimed.

"Why hasn't anyone made an announcement? This moment should not go unnoticed."

"You afraid I'll back out if there aren't witnesses?" Laila teased.

"Well, you have been known to get cold feet about this relationship before," Jess said.

"But today it all became very clear to me. Matthew is the future I want. No more doubts. No questions. No hiding," Laila said firmly.

"Well, hallelujah for that," Connie said. "How did it happen?"

"Was it when he got you alone after church last night?" Jess asked. "That get-lost look he gave Will and me was pretty obvious."

Laila described how badly that plan had fallen through and how quickly they'd gotten naked afterward.

"Too much information," Jess protested, then studied her. "But if not then, when?"

"This morning," Laila said, then grinned at the memory. "In bed. I said yes right after telling my father once and for all that I didn't want his stupid bank job. I was pretty darn proud of myself."

"My, my, you *have* had yourself quite a Christmas morning, and it's barely daylight over here," Jess said. "When are you going to tell everyone, and what about the wedding? Is it going to be here?"

"Matthew's convinced we can pull it off," Laila admitted. "I've agreed to let Nell try to work her magic."

"This is absolutely the best family ever," Connie said with enthusiasm. "I'm so glad I'm a part of it."

"Speaking of big news, have you shared yours with Thomas?" Laila asked Connie.

A smile split her friend's face. "I have, and you should have seen him. He went white with shock for a minute, then spun me around the room till I was dizzy. I think he's having trouble keeping it to himself. He's barely spoken to a soul all morning for fear he'll slip."

"I can imagine what torture it must be for him to keep quiet about this. It's definitely not his nature to keep such wonderful news to himself," Jess said.

"Well, he promised," Connie said. "I don't want Jenny spoiling things with some sort of tantrum."

"And why would I be throwing a tantrum?" Jenny inquired, approaching from behind just in time to overhear.

Connie went pale.

"Tell her," Jess advised, giving Connie's hand a reassuring squeeze. "We're here if you need us."

She and Laila walked away.

"Let's not go far in case Connie needs us," Laila said, her gaze on the mother and daughter who were deep in an obviously tense conversation.

Jenny's shocked gaze sought out Thomas, who was rapidly making his way toward them. Apparently his radar had alerted him to Connie's distress.

"Oh, boy," Jess whispered.

Thomas put one arm around Connie's shoulders. He started to put the other around Jenny, but she shrugged it away, an expression of betrayal on her face.

"What's that about?" Matthew asked, joining Laila and Jess.

Laila looked to Jess. "Any reason not to tell him now?"

"Not that I can think of," Jess said, then threw her

arms around Matthew. "Congratulations, by the way! Let me know what I can do to help with the wedding."

"Believe me, we'll be in touch," Matthew responded. "We have something like forty-eight hours to pull it off."

"Two days?" Laila said when they were alone. Even though she'd agreed, she was a little daunted by the reality of such a timetable.

"It's going to be fine," Matthew assured her. "Now, tell me what's up with Uncle Thomas and Connie that has Jenny looking like she's ready to explode."

"Connie's pregnant," Laila said excitedly. "Isn't that incredible?"

Matthew's eyes lit up. "It *is* incredible. Good for them. I suppose now would be a bad time to offer my congratulations."

"I think we need to give Jenny some time to get used to the idea," Laila said. "At least she hasn't bolted out of here and caused a scene."

"Think maybe we should seize the moment with our own announcement?" he asked. "That ought to stir things up and give Thomas and Connie a breather from their drama."

"Now?" she asked, suddenly hesitant.

"Sweetheart, if we're going to be married in two days and you keep flashing that ring around, we don't have a lot of time to keep this to ourselves. We need everyone in this room on board. I suspect someone already has a clipboard with a list of everything that needs to happen and assignments to be sure it all gets done."

Laila glanced around in search of her brother. "Maybe I should tell Trace first."

"I've spoken to him. He knows and he's already on the case with your parents."

"Thank you for opening the door to them being here," she said. "I know I invited them, but I think it will actually mean a lot if Trace can tell them that you want them here, too."

Matthew regarded her worriedly. "Don't get your hopes up, okay?"

"I know. It would be weird to get married without having them here, but it's their decision. If they stay away, it's their loss."

He squeezed her hand. "It really is, you know. You're going to be the most beautiful bride in the entire world."

There was a gasp behind them.

"Did I hear someone mention a bride?" Jo O'Brien asked, her eyes alight with excitement. "Laila, have you finally said yes to my son?"

Laila nodded, only to find herself engulfed in Jo's strong embrace.

"Thank goodness," Jo said. "I was so afraid Matthew's powers of persuasion were going to fail him this time."

"Oh, I think he has that particular skill nailed," Laila said wryly.

Matthew shook his head. "Since the news seems to be leaking out bit by bit, I'm going to make it official before everyone else steals my thunder."

Because the level of noise in the room was out of control, he actually climbed onto a chair, then coaxed Laila up there with him, his arms tight around her waist as she leaned back against his chest.

"Hey, everyone! Merry Christmas," he shouted. "Could I have your attention for a minute?"

Murmurs spread through the room.

Matthew laughed. "Oh, stop your speculating, everyone! A couple of hours ago, this amazing woman consented to be my wife."

Shouts rose up, along with a few teasing jeers about Laila's apparent lack of good sense. The latter came mostly from Luke. A scowl from Matthew and an admonishment from Moira silenced him.

"Before you ask, the wedding date is day after tomorrow, if we can pull it off," he announced, then glanced around at the room until his gaze settled on Nell. "Think that's possible, Gram?"

"I guarantee it," Nell said, grinning.

"A toast," Jeff O'Brien called out. "To my son for showing the good sense to fight for the woman he loves, and to Laila for being brave enough to join this family!"

"To Matthew and Laila!" echoed around the room.

Laila looked into Matthew's eyes and saw all the love she could possibly ever want there.

"You are brave, you know," he said softly before helping her down to face the crowd of well-wishers.

Laila smiled. There it was again, another trait she'd never realized she possessed: bravery.

"Only because you've made me that way," she told him.

"We're going to be good together," he promised.

"Better than good," she corrected. "We're going to be amazing."

Epilogue

The O'Brien elves, given a deadline, worked harder than any in Santa's workshop. Laila was in awe of them. Though the day after Christmas in Dublin was another holiday, calls were made, doors opened, dresses were showcased, flowers ordered and a special license delivered, thanks to Gram's persistence and Connor's legal expertise.

Even the priest, after initial reservations, agreed the circumstances were such that a few rules could be bent. Apparently his predecessor had had very fond memories of Nell's family and spoken highly of their many kindnesses before he'd passed on. It didn't hurt that Dillon's tobacco shop seemed to be a favorite of his, as well.

Kiera and even Moira got into the spirit of things and proved themselves indispensable, running errands, making calls, even stitching the necessary alterations to the dress that Laila had loved.

"Are you sure there's time?" Laila had asked worriedly.

"For a few nips and tucks? Of course," Kiera said readily. "The dress will fit like a dream by tomorrow. No worries."

And it did, Laila conceded, gazing into a mirror in the dressing room at the church. Though Kiera continued to fuss over a few final details, the slim column of satin was perfect, leaving her shoulders bare and caressing her slender body like a glove. It had only the barest puddle of shimmering white as a train at her feet.

Bree had huddled with the neighborhood florist, another friend of Dillon's, to create a simple bouquet of white orchids and trailing dark green ribbons that matched exactly the cocktail-length green dresses they'd found for Jess and Connie, who were dual matrons of honor. Luke and Mack would be standing up with Matthew, tiny white orchids on the lapels of their hastily tailored tuxedos.

It was to be an evening service, with the old church lit with candles as it had been on Christmas Eve. Bree had freshened the flowers from the holiday services, adding the perfect touches to make them special without the necessity for a lot of tedious work that there was no time for and that Laila had declared wasteful in light of the beauty of the existing arrangements.

Carrie and Caitlyn, who'd once declared themselves the family's designated flower girls and more recently insisted on bridesmaid status, had chosen their own dresses in a green tartan plaid taffeta, with dark green sashes that matched the ribbons in the flowers and the matron of honor dresses. Though she'd imagined a much simpler event, given the time constraints, Laila had been unable to ignore her stepnieces' entreaties to be a part of her big day.

Now the twins were bubbling with excitement, and Connie and Jess were fussing over the tiara and short veil Laila had chosen. Every time they rearranged it, the finicky hairdresser insisted on giving her hair another touch-up. Even Abby had come back to check on their progress, so the dressing room was delightfully chaotic, allowing little time to think of the person who wasn't there—her own mother.

When Jo arrived and caught sight of Laila, her eyes lit up, then immediately filled with tears. "Oh, Laila, you look absolutely stunning. I really do wish…"

Though her voice trailed off, Laila knew what she'd wanted to say. She, too, wished that her mother was here, fretting over every detail. She squeezed Jo's hand. "It's okay," she said. "I'm marrying Matthew and gaining you for a mother-in-law. How could I possibly be any happier?"

"Do you mind if Susie comes back?" Jo asked. "She's feeling very proprietary about bringing the two of you back together."

"Of course she can come back," Laila said, even though she was beginning to feel overwhelmed by all the attention. She'd need a bit of breathing room soon, if she wasn't to panic.

Susie came into the room moments later, took one look at Laila and burst into tears.

Laila rushed to embrace her, as did Jess and Connie. "What is it?" Jess asked. "Sweetie, are you okay?"

"I'm fine," Susie insisted, though her chin wobbled

and tears continued to spill down her cheeks as she managed a watery smile for Laila. "This is exactly what I wanted for you, and I am so, so happy for you and my brother."

Laila studied her knowingly. "But you're thinking that you and Mack never did have a proper wedding, aren't you?"

"We had a huge party," Susie reminded her, then nodded. "But yes, I'm thinking about everything the cancer cost us. I always dreamed about the big hoopla."

"You can still have it," Laila assured her.

"Of course you can," Jess said. "We'll plan it the minute we get back home. We'll do it in celebration of your first anniversary. You can walk down the aisle in a Vera Wang gown, if that's what you want. We'll make sure it costs Uncle Jeff a fortune!"

Susie gave them a grateful smile, even as Jess dabbed away her tears. "You guys are the absolute best," she said, then regarded Laila apologetically. "I'm so sorry. I didn't mean to come back here and be this big downer. I had no idea seeing you like this would have such an effect on me."

Laila smiled at her. "I don't think a few tears could possibly spoil this day for me. And planning the big, fancy ceremony that you and Mack deserve will give us all something to look forward to. From what I've seen, there's nothing O'Briens love more than a party and an excuse to celebrate."

"Absolutely," Jess said, then grinned. "And all these family occasions and receptions are fantastic business for my inn, so I'm all for them."

Connie glanced at her watch. "I hate to ruin this

lovely bonding moment, but it's time, ladies. Abby, can you corral your daughters? If we don't start down the aisle on time, Matthew's likely to have a coronary. He seemed a little anxious last time I saw him."

Susie laughed. "Anxious doesn't begin to describe it. He's a wreck. I'll go alert him that his moments as a bachelor are numbered."

After she and Abby had gone, Jess and Connie turned to Laila.

"Ready?" Jess asked.

Laila drew in a deep breath, then nodded. She was shaky, but confident. This was everything she'd ever wanted.

"Okay, then," Connie said. "Let's get this show on the road. I'm so glad you decided not to waste time and agreed to do this today."

Laila regarded her with amusement. "Why is that?"

"Because in no time, I'll be big as a house, and there wouldn't have been a dress in the entire bridal universe that I could have worn down the aisle. This one's already starting to feel a little snug."

Jess shook her head. "Babies don't grow that quickly," she told her. "That's the double serving of eggs, toast and sausages you had for breakfast and the fish-and-chips you had for lunch."

Connie laughed. "Could be," she said easily. "I still think we need to hurry."

Laila followed them to the church vestibule, where Carrie and Caitlyn were already waiting. She looked around for Trace, who'd agreed to walk her down the aisle, but instead it was her father who stepped out of the shadows. Her breath caught in her throat at the sight of him, looking so incredibly handsome in his tux, his gaze wary as he approached her.

"Dad?" she said, as if she couldn't trust her eyes.

"Need an escort?" he asked, his expression solemn.

Laila's eyes filled with tears, which Jess rushed forward to dab before they could ruin her makeup. Apparently she'd assigned herself to be the keeper of the tissues today.

"You came," Laila said, her choked voice filled with wonder as she looked at her father. "I can't believe it. You really came."

"How could we miss our only daughter's wedding?" he asked. "Trace made it clear we'd never forgive ourselves if we did, and for once your brother was right. This is where your mother and I had to be today. And, so you know, Matthew and I've made peace, as well. He made a strong case for how much he loves you, and I have to respect him for that. This marriage will take a bit of getting used to, but we owe you our unconditional support."

That came as an even bigger—and more welcome— shock than his presence. "I'm so glad," she said. "You can't begin to know what having you here means to me."

He smiled at her, his own eyes misty. "I think maybe I do," he said. "Because it means the world to me that you wanted us here after all I've put you through."

"In the past," she said, determined to make it so. "Please, Dad, can we agree to leave it in the past?"

"It's all forgotten," he said, then drew her arm through his. "I imagine Matthew's wondering what's taking so long. Let's not keep him waiting."

At some signal she didn't see, the music began and

Carrie and Caitlyn started down the aisle, an eager bounce in their steps.

Jess and Connie gave Laila a wink, then followed.

Laila looked into her father's eyes.

"You ready?" he asked.

"I've never been more ready for anything," she assured him.

He nodded. "Then that's all that matters to me," he told her gently, giving her hand a pat.

With her father at her side, Laila was blind to everyone except Matthew as she made her way to the front of the church. Only at the last second did she spot her mother, openly weeping in the front pew. For the second time, Laila's eyes filled, but she blinked away the tears, then turned to Matthew, this man who'd helped her discover the woman she could be.

"I love you," he mouthed just before they turned to face the priest.

And with the solemn words of the ceremony echoing through the church, their future began.

Matthew clasped Laila's hand reassuringly in his. With his warmth and love flowing through her, she knew their future was going to be everything she'd ever dreamed of, and that no matter how many wonderful Christmas memories they made in the years to come, this one would always be the very best.

* * * * *

Look for Sherryl Woods's next reissue, AFTER TEX, coming in January 2013, and her next original novel, SAND CASTLE BAY, available in May 2013.

Based on the popular *Sweet Magnolias* series comes

THE SWEET MAGNOLIAS COOKBOOK

New York Times and USA TODAY Bestselling Author
SHERRYL WOODS
WITH CHEF TEDDI WOHLFORD

The
SWEET MAGNOLIAS
Cookbook

MORE THAN 100 FAVORITE SOUTHERN RECIPES

From
The Sweet Magnolias Cookbook!

Fire & Ice Pickles

2 (32-ounce) jars nonrefrigerated pickle slices
4 cups granulated sugar
2 tablespoons Tabasco sauce

1 teaspoon crushed red pepper flakes
4 minced garlic cloves

1. Combine all ingredients, and mix well.

2. Cover, and let stand at room temperature 3–4 hours, stirring occasionally.

3. Divide into 4 (1-pint) canning jars. Seal tightly.

4. Refrigerate up to 1 month.

Note: Best if made at least 1 week before eating to allow flavors to develop.

MAKES 4 PINTS.

Available September 2012! Order your copy today!

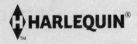

HNSMCBMM

New York Times bestselling author

SHERRYL WOODS

continues her delightful Sweet Magnolia series
with three new stories!

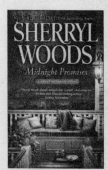 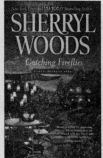 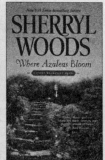

Available wherever books are sold!

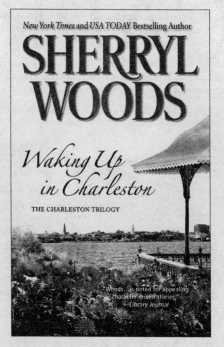

#1 *NEW YORK TIMES* BESTSELLING AUTHOR

ROBYN CARR

Patrick Riordan has always been the sweet-natured one in his family. These days, his easygoing manner is being tested by his career as a navy pilot. But for the Riordan brothers, when the going gets tough…the tough find the love of a good woman.

Angie LeCroix comes to Virgin River to spend Christmas away from her hovering mother. Yet instead of freedom, she gets Jack Sheridan. If her uncle had his way, she'd never go out again. And certainly not with rugged, handsome Patrick Riordan.

When sparks start to fly, Patrick and Angie just want to be left alone together. But their families have different plans for them—and for Christmas, Virgin River style!

MY KIND *of* CHRISTMAS

REQUEST YOUR FREE BOOKS!

2 FREE NOVELS
FROM THE ROMANCE COLLECTION
PLUS 2 FREE GIFTS!

YES! Please send me 2 FREE novels from the Romance Collection and my 2 FREE gifts (gifts are worth about $10). After receiving them, if I don't wish to receive any more books, I can return the shipping statement marked "cancel." If I don't cancel, I will receive 4 brand-new novels every month and be billed just $5.99 per book in the U.S. or $6.49 per book in Canada. That's a saving of at least 25% off the cover price. It's quite a bargain! Shipping and handling is just 50¢ per book in the U.S. and 75¢ per book in Canada.* I understand that accepting the 2 free books and gifts places me under no obligation to buy anything. I can always return a shipment and cancel at any time. Even if I never buy another book, the two free books and gifts are mine to keep forever.

194/394 MDN FELQ

Name	(PLEASE PRINT)	

Address		Apt. #

City	State/Prov.	Zip/Postal Code

Signature (if under 18, a parent or guardian must sign)

Mail to the **Reader Service:**
IN U.S.A.: P.O. Box 1867, Buffalo, NY 14240-1867
IN CANADA: P.O. Box 609, Fort Erie, Ontario L2A 5X3

Not valid for current subscribers to the Romance Collection
or the Romance/Suspense Collection.

Want to try two free books from another line?
Call 1-800-873-8635 or visit www.ReaderService.com.

* Terms and prices subject to change without notice. Prices do not include applicable taxes. Sales tax applicable in N.Y. Canadian residents will be charged applicable taxes. Offer not valid in Quebec. This offer is limited to one order per household. All orders subject to credit approval. Credit or debit balances in a customer's account(s) may be offset by any other outstanding balance owed by or to the customer. Please allow 4 to 6 weeks for delivery. Offer available while quantities last.

Your Privacy—The Reader Service is committed to protecting your privacy. Our Privacy Policy is available online at www.ReaderService.com or upon request from the Reader Service.

We make a portion of our mailing list available to reputable third parties that offer products we believe may interest you. If you prefer that we not exchange your name with third parties, or if you wish to clarify or modify your communication preferences, please visit us at www.ReaderService.com/consumerschoice or write to us at Reader Service Preference Service, P.O. Box 9062, Buffalo, NY 14269. Include your complete name and address.

ROM11

SHEILA ROBERTS

Cass Wilkes, owner of the Gingerbread Haus bakery in Icicle Falls, was looking forward to her daughter Danielle's holiday wedding. But every B and B is full, and it looks as if Danielle's father, his trophy wife and their yappy little dog will be staying with Cass.

Her friend Charlene Albach has just seen the ghost of Christmas past: her ex-husband, Richard, who ran off a year ago with the hostess from *her* restaurant. Now the hostess is history and he wants to kiss and make up. Hide the mistletoe!

Then there's Ella O'Brien, who's newly divorced but still living with her ex—and still fighting as though they were married. The love is gone. Isn't it?

But Christmas has a way of working its magic. Merry Ex-mas, ladies!

Available wherever books are sold.

HARLEQUIN® MIRA®

™ www.Harlequin.com

MSR1392

SHERRYL WOODS

(limited quantities available)

TOTAL AMOUNT	$ _____
POSTAGE & HANDLING	$ _____
($1.00 for 1 book, 50¢ for each additional)	
APPLICABLE TAXES*	$ _____
TOTAL PAYABLE	$ _____

(check or money order—please do not send cash)

To order, complete this form and send it, along with a check or money order for the total above, payable to Harlequin MIRA, to: **In the U.S.:** 3010 Walden Avenue, P.O. Box 9077, Buffalo, NY 14269-9077; **In Canada:** P.O. Box 636, Fort Erie, Ontario, L2A 5X3.

Name: _____

Address: _____ City: _____

State/Prov.: _____ Zip/Postal Code: _____

Account Number (if applicable): _____

075 CSAS

*New York residents remit applicable sales taxes.
*Canadian residents remit applicable GST and provincial taxes.

H HARLEQUIN® MIRA®

™ www.Harlequin.com

MSW1112BL